THE HONOR OF LAWRENCE HOUSE

The Honor
of Lawrence House

by
VIRGINIA DAILEY

DUELL, SLOAN AND PEARCE
New York

Dailey, Virginia.   The honor of Lawrence House.   [1st ed.]   New York,
   Duell, Sloan and Pearce [1959]   181 p.   22 cm.   1. Title.   PZ7.D152Ho
   813.5   59–5559 ‡   Library of Congress

First edition

Manufactured in the United States of America

VAN REES PRESS • NEW YORK

To my parents

EDGAR *and* ALICE POE

Contents

1. On Campus!   3

2. The Lawrence Girls   12

3. Kitchen Boy   23

4. The Speech Clinic   37

5. An Afternoon at Howley's   47

6. The Valentine Day Dance   59

7. A Bracelet Disappears   71

8. Enter a Movie Queen   84

9. A Surprise for Rosemary   96

10. Thad Asks a Favor   113

11. A Mystery Solved   126

12. Rosemary Reveals a Secret   139

13. May Wedding   156

14. Awards Day   163

15. Till September   174

THE HONOR OF LAWRENCE HOUSE

On Campus!

ROSEMARY ROSSITER CHECKED HER BAGS IN THE BUS STATION at Waverly and started off across the Waverly College campus, which was in the center of the small town. As she walked along, Rosemary looked about with interest. The original administration building was faded red brick, almost obscured by the heavy tendrils of ivy that clung to its walls. Now the college had a dozen modern buildings and a student body of more than three thousand.

It was conservative and democratic, according to the catalogue, which Rosemary had studied so avidly, for it forbade social fraternities and sororities. All of the students resided in dormitories, boarded in private homes, or lived in one of the private houses.

Her uncle Leon had told Rosemary that Lawrence House, where she was to live, was one of Waverly's most beloved traditions. The residents were usually daughters of Lawrence alumni or girls who had been recommended by Lawrence alumni. Rosemary's aunt Caroline had been a Lawrence girl, and she and Uncle Leon had met when he attended Waverly's Agricultural School.

Rosemary noticed a girl ahead of her getting out of a car. She kissed an older couple, presumably her parents, good-by.

It reminded Rosemary of her own leave-taking when she had kissed her mother at the bus station. "I'm going to be dreadfully homesick, I know, Mother," she had said mournfully. She couldn't admit even to her mother that she was scared, deep down scared.

Her mother had rubbed her cheek against Rosemary's. "You may at first, dear, but after you get acquainted, you'll forget all about being homesick," Frances Rossiter had said comfortingly. "And don't worry about me. I'll be all right. I have lots of interesting plans made."

Rosemary had watched until the bus was out of sight and she could no longer see her mother's small figure waving good-by on the platform. She shed a few quiet tears into her handkerchief. She wondered if she were making a mistake even going off to college. Pangs of doubt assailed her again. She was so average she didn't excel in anything. In fact, she didn't even know what she wanted to do, or what she wanted to major in.

A sign pointed to the gymnasium as the place of registration, and Rosemary went inside. Everyone seemed to be wandering around looking at signs. She finally located the one that said "Incoming Freshmen" and gave her name to the student behind the desk. The student found her class cards and told Rosemary to fill them out at a table in the middle of the gymnasium.

As she filled in the innumerable cards, Rosemary thought that she was glad all liberal-arts students had to take a general course the first year. By then she should know what she wanted to major in. Besides, she wasn't even sure now she would be able to return for a second semester, so a general course would be the most useful.

After she had completed her registration, Rosemary went out into the crisp air again. Now on to Lawrence House. She picked up her luggage at the bus station and walked back across the campus. The tree branches were weighted down by the heavy snow that had fallen during the night. The walks were cleared but snow was banked at the edges, making a white-walled path.

According to her uncle's directions, Lawrence House faced the campus at the far end. A large white frame house, he had said, colonial style, with white pillars. Rosemary found it without difficulty. It was quite impressive-looking, she thought. An American flag fluttered on a tall pole above the porch. There was a neatly lettered small gold sign on the lawn, "Lawrence House."

Rosemary rang the doorbell and heard a masculine voice say, "Come in." She opened the door, and a man sitting at a table in the hall rose promptly. He was erect and spare with white hair and a trim goatee. He wore gold-rimmed spectacles, a high white collar, and a black string tie, reminding Rosemary of photographs she had seen of Victorian gentlemen.

"How do you do, young lady?" he said in a surprisingly deep voice. "I'm Irving Lawrence. May I help you?"

"I'm Rosemary Rossiter, Mr. Lawrence," she said timidly.

He shook hands with her formally. "Oh, yes, Leon and Caroline's niece," he said. "I'm glad you have arrived safely, Miss Rossiter. Won't you step into my office? I have a record card for you to fill out before we go upstairs." He showed her into a tiny office not much larger than a closet, where he had a file cabinet, a small desk, and two chairs.

Rosemary looked at Mr. Lawrence with undisguised interest. She had never seen a man before with a goatee, except in the movies, but she found herself liking him at once. Mr. Lawrence handed Rosemary a file card that inquired into her personal data, her hobbies, and her likes and dislikes in foods. "I have these cards on all my young ladies for the thirty-five years I've been here," he explained. "Would you please fill it out, Miss Rossiter?"

Rosemary filled out the card, unaware that Irving Lawrence was studying her with amazingly perceptive eyes behind his spectacles. He saw a slender girl with deep brown eyes, naturally curly brown hair, and a rather diffident manner that was more appealing than she realized.

When Rosemary finished, he said, "Your roommate will be Esther Mercer, Miss Rossiter. I think you'll like her. Her room was the only one with a vacancy because her roommate left at the end of the first semester." He paused and asked kindly, "Do you have any questions?"

Rosemary pondered and then shook her head. "No, sir. I believe not; everything seems clear."

"All right, then, I'll show you your room, Miss Rossiter." Mr. Lawrence picked up her bags and showed her up the winding staircase to the second floor. They walked along the hall and Mr. Lawrence opened the door into the last room on the right.

"You may put your things away, Miss Rossiter. Miss Mercer cleared her clothes out of half of the closet." He set her bags on one of the beds. "This side of the room is yours."

The room was large, with three windows that faced out over the street and overlooked the campus. The bedspreads were a gay red plaid and matching draw draperies hung at the windows. Each girl had a dresser, a worktable with a bronze reading lamp on it, a small bookcase, a lounge chair, and a straight chair. A large closet with double sliding doors was at one end of the room. A green grass rug made a startling contrast with the red plaid.

Rosemary turned to Mr. Lawrence. "It's a lovely room, sir," she said.

He looked pleased. "I'm glad you like it, my dear. I hope you are happy here."

Neither of them had heard footsteps. They both started as they heard the unexpected voice behind them. A tall honey-blonde, with her hair arranged in a pony tail, stood looking in the door. "Are you Rosemary?" she asked pleasantly. "I'm your house president, Alicia Barnes."

"Miss Barnes, Miss Rossiter," Mr. Lawrence said, with a courtly bow toward Alicia. The two girls smiled at each other. "Miss Barnes is a senior, Miss Rossiter," he explained. "She has been with me the longest of any of the present girls."

"I'll explain the house rules, Rosemary," Alicia said. "My room is at the other end of the hall. I'll talk with you later after Mr. Lawrence is finished." She nodded and went off down the hall.

Alicia Barnes, Rosemary repeated to herself, fixing the name in her mind. She had admired the girl's well-cut suit and her immaculate grooming. Oh, dear, she thought nervously, I hope all the girls aren't that pretty and well dressed. I'll feel terribly out of place.

Mr. Lawrence told her supper would be at six o'clock and went off downstairs. Rosemary put her clothes away, and then she stretched out on the bed. She had not realized until now how tired she was. For a few moments she reviewed her new experiences and the people she had already met. Before she knew it, she had dropped off to sleep.

Rosemary was awakened by the sound of someone moving about the room. It was almost dark outside now and the lamp was lit on Esther's dresser.

The girl at the mirror turned when she heard Rosemary stirring. She was tiny, at least a head shorter than Rosemary, with a childlike face, wide china-blue eyes, and blond hair, which she wore in a brief gamin bob.

"Oh, hi, you must be Rosemary," she said in a friendly manner. "I'm Esther Mercer, your roommate. I hope you like the room, Rosemary."

Rosemary shook her head to wipe away the cobwebs left from her nap. "Hello, Esther. I must have slept longer than I realized." She was embarrassed that her new roommate had found her asleep the first thing. She must think her a perfect dolt.

Esther was applying fresh make-up. She nodded over her shoulder. "Think nothing of it. Registration does that to everybody, Rosemary. I'm simply dead myself, but I didn't finish in time to take a nap. You were lucky to get through so fast."

"I started early," Rosemary explained. "Are you a freshman, too, Esther?" she asked. She watched Esther arching her eyebrows and applying a brown eyebrow pencil. She's a cute little trick, Rosemary thought, like a little doll rather than a college girl. Oh, I hope she likes me! Everyone says it's so important to have a congenial roommate. I hope I didn't disappoint her.

"Second-semester freshman," Esther replied, leaning

8

closer to the mirror and touching her eyelashes with a tiny brush. "You'll like it at Waverly, Rosemary. Lots of activities and social affairs. And, believe it or not, the boys outnumber the girls. The Agriculture School, you know."

"That's good news," Rosemary said. "Is your home here in town, Esther?"

"No, my folks live in Freesburg, but I like being off by myself. You'll like it, too, when you get used to it."

Rosemary thought of her mother, and a sharp pang of homesickness flashed through her. Frances Rossiter would just be coming home to the empty, dark house and preparing her supper to be eaten alone.

"How'd you happen to enter Waverly in the middle of the year, Rosemary?" Esther asked curiously.

"I had enough credits so I decided to finish high school the first semester," Rosemary replied. She had hoped to be of some help to her mother by getting a job. But there had been no jobs in Farmingdale after the holidays. If Uncle Leon hadn't come forward with his welcome offer, Rosemary would still be sitting around the house.

Alicia Barnes stuck her head in the door again. "I see you finally woke up, Rosemary," she said. "I stopped in awhile ago, but you were so sound asleep I didn't have the heart to awaken you. Come on down to my room so we won't bore Esther. She's heard all this before."

Esther replied, "You can say that again, Alicia. You're going to get the works, Rosemary."

Rosemary hadn't had a chance to freshen her appearance after her nap, but she was too shy to tell Alicia. She followed her to the end room which was exactly like her own except that the spreads and draperies were blue plaid instead of red. Alicia motioned for Rosemary to sit down in the lounge chair. She lit a cigarette and offered Rosemary one, but she declined politely. Her mother disapproved of girls smoking, so she had never smoked.

"There aren't a lot of hard-and-fast rules here, Rosemary," Alicia began. She had a precise, crisp manner of speaking. Rosemary could see why she would be selected house president. Everything about her bespoke efficiency and orderliness. "But the college does have certain policies for all of the houses and dormitories. Lights out at ten except Saturday nights, and then midnight. No evening dates during the week for freshmen and sophomores. Friday and Saturday nights are date nights. Of course, no boys upstairs. You can bring your date into the lounge. You have to share in keeping your room clean. Meals are at regular hours. You must be on time, or you earn demerits. You'll find the schedules and menus posted downstairs on the bulletin board in the hall." She paused and looked at Rosemary, as though she expected questions.

"What about Mr. Lawrence, Alicia?" Rosemary asked. "Does he pay any attention to what we do?"

Alicia smiled. "He knows everything that's going on, Rosemary, believe me, even though he does live on the first floor. But he doesn't say much usually. If he has any complaints about a girl's actions, he speaks to me first about it, and I speak to the girl. If matters don't improve, he calls the girl in and has one of his desk-side chats. I suppose you've already heard about the glory of old Lawrence House. It's a campus institution, you know." Her tone was light but there was an underlying note of seriousness in it.

"Yes, I have, Alicia," Rosemary said. "I really feel honored to be living there." The old pangs of insecurity seized her. Would she be able to fit into the pattern expected of her as a Lawrence girl? A pattern of thirty-five years of outstanding girls?

Alicia tapped out her cigarette with an economy of movement. "If anything comes up that troubles you, Rosemary, come in and talk it over. Most freshmen are homesick for a while, so don't be ashamed if you are, too. You're free to go home weekends if you wish—just so you sign out when you leave and are back in the house by ten Sunday night."

She rose and smoothed her neat skirt. She made Rosemary feel all thumbs and big feet. "I think that covers everything, Rosemary. It's nearly suppertime. Want to go downstairs and I'll introduce you around?"

Rosemary said she'd be down as soon as she rinsed her face and combed her hair. She dashed back to her room. Esther was gone and Rosemary was glad of the chance to get herself together before meeting the other girls.

In a few moments she joined Alicia in the pleasant chintz-decorated lounge on the side of the hall across from Mr. Lawrence's office. Rosemary had a quick impression of all different sizes, shapes, and types of girls. They all glanced up expectantly as Rosemary and Alicia entered. She felt a dryness in her mouth at being the object of so much attention. She could feel her cheeks burning and her knees knocking. She wished she were back home in Farmingdale.

CHAPTER 2

The Lawrence Girls

ALICIA STARTED IN THE NEAR CORNER WHERE A DARK-HAIRED, stout girl was writing what looked like a theme. She had a round, plain face and unbecoming long bangs. Her horn-rimmed glasses gave her a studious air. Rosemary pasted a stiff smile on her lips, trying to appear more at ease than she actually was.

"This is Donna Farrell, one of our brightest intellectual hopes," Alicia said, turning to Rosemary. "Donna's here on a scholarship and lives directly across the hall from you. Her roommate is Lee Ann Meadows."

Donna stood up, shook hands with Rosemary, and murmured a few polite words of welcome. As soon as they passed by, she immediately became engrossed again in her work. Rosemary breathed a little more easily. This wasn't quite so bad as she had expected. Donna certainly wasn't much to look at.

"And this is Lee Ann Meadows," Alicia said, "Rosemary Rossiter."

The brown-haired girl sitting on the window seat staring off into space was pretty but had a rather wistful expression, Rosemary thought. She was wearing an expensive-looking beige wool dress. When Alicia spoke, she turned with an absent-minded air, as though suddenly brought back to earth, and murmured in a low, well-bred voice, "Welcome to Lawrence House, Rosemary."

Alicia added casually, "Lee Ann is a celebrity's daughter, Rosemary. Her mother is Melissa Meadows."

Rosemary was surprised by the almost anguished expression that flashed momentarily across Lee Ann's face and then was gone. Melissa Meadows, she remembered reading in a column just last week, was honeymooning in Europe with her fourth husband before beginning her next movie. "I've seen a lot of your mother's movies, Lee Ann," Rosemary said, thinking it the courteous thing to say.

Lee Ann shrugged slightly and murmured, "Have you?" in a disinterested voice. Rosemary got the immediate impression that Lee Ann wasn't too much interested in her mother's movie career.

They moved on across the room where two girls were arguing about the comparative merits of studying French versus Spanish. They ceased when Alicia and Rosemary approached. One girl was jolly-looking with carroty-red hair, shining hazel eyes, and a wide mouth. She had a generous sprinkling of freckles on her uptilted nose.

Alicia said, "This is Nancy Potter, Rosemary. Nancy's the live wire of the house." Rosemary instantly liked the bright-faced girl who emanated vitality and good humor.

"Hi, Rosemary. Don't believe everything Alicia tells you," Nancy said. "She thinks I'm a giddy influence around here." But it was said good-naturedly, and it was obvious no one took it seriously, least of all Alicia.

The other girl lifted her eyebrows in an aloof manner. She was startlingly beautiful with soft white skin, a clear-cut Grecian profile, and black hair swept back in wings from a middle part. She stared at Rosemary, taking her in from head to foot. Rosemary had the uncomfortable feeling that her slip must be showing. She glanced down at herself and wished she had worn something other than this old black sweater.

"I take it this is our new little freshman," the beautiful girl said, as though she had summed up Rosemary and found her wanting.

"Yes, this is Beverly Coleman, Rosemary Rossiter," Alicia answered hastily. "Beverly's the only junior in the house and rooms with me."

Rosemary murmured a courteous greeting, but there was something about the other girl she didn't quite cotton to, an air of arrogance which spoiled her flawless facial beauty.

Alicia whispered as they passed on, "Avery Coleman, the oil magnate, you know. Beverly's his one precious offspring. She's rather on the snooty side, but all right when you get to know her." Rosemary nodded, but she reserved judgment. She had the feeling Beverly didn't think much of her.

Just then another girl with a harried expression came flying into the lounge. She wore no make-up and her hair was drawn back tightly in a stiff bun. Her gray dress had long sleeves and a high neck. Rosemary thought that she looked just like the Puritan girls in the history books.

"Something wrong, Fern?" Alicia asked, approaching the newcomer, for the girl was looking around the room anxiously.

"Has Wilma come in yet?" Fern asked.

"I haven't seen her, Fern," Alicia replied. "Why?"

Fern shook her head disapprovingly. "Wilma left registration with some boy and said she'd be back in time for supper. Now she's not here!" Her voice rose to a high pitch. "You know Mr. Lawrence said if Wilma was late one more time, he'd have to penalize her." Her light gray eyes blinked rapidly and she stared at Rosemary as though just noticing her. Fern surely is a different type from the other Lawrence girls, Rosemary thought.

"Oh, excuse me. This is our new freshman, Fern," Alicia said, remembering her manners. "Rosemary Rossiter, Fern Waterman. Fern's a sophomore and Wilma Nastri's roommate, Rosemary." Alicia lowered her voice and spoke soothingly to Fern. "It isn't your worry, Fern. You know how Wilma is."

"I certainly do, Alicia!" Fern snapped. "If a boy comes in sight, she's off. I never saw such a silly girl. I declare, I don't know what to do with her!"

Alicia lifted her left eyebrow toward Rosemary and her lips twitched slightly. Rosemary had to repress a smile herself. Fern was rather comic even though she was deadly serious.

Just then a dinner bell chimed softly and all the girls rose. At the same moment the front door banged and a girl came panting into the hall. She was disheveled and bright-cheeked. "Am I . . . too late, Alicia?" she gasped.

"Just in time, Wilma," Alicia replied calmly. "Take off your coat and leave it in here before Mr. Lawrence catches you again."

Hastily the girl dropped her coat on a chair and tried to smooth down her wind-blown hair. "I ran . . . all the way . . . from Howley's," she explained between gasps.

15

"You're just lucky, Wilma," Fern said sharply. "The next time you'll get caught and you know what that means."

Wilma ignored this thrust and smiled blithely. She was an attractive girl, Rosemary thought, but she wore a trifle too much make-up and would undoubtedly be termed "fast" in Farmingdale.

Wilma looked speculatively at Rosemary. "I don't know you, do I?" she asked.

Alicia made the introductions. "You look like a nice kid," Wilma said. "Just don't get in with the wrong crowd, that's all." She glanced pointedly at Fern, who was chewing her lip in stern concentration.

"I'll try not to, Wilma," Rosemary said politely. What an oddly assorted pair of roommates, she thought. "Have I met everyone now?" she asked Alicia as they went into the long, candlelit dining room.

"Everyone but Cynthia Sanders, a girl from my home town," Alicia replied. "She's in the infirmary with the flu."

After Mr. Lawrence had said grace, Rosemary looked around the table and repeated the name of each girl to herself. How pretty they all looked in the candlelight. It was even flattering to the colorless Fern. Rosemary wondered what the girls thought of her. Everyone had seemed pleasant except Beverly Coleman. Rosemary had the feeling they would never become close friends, for Beverly was the type of girl who always made Rosemary feel frumpy and inept.

After supper the girls drifted out of the dining room one by one. Not knowing what else to do, Rosemary returned to her room. Classes would begin in the morning. She was looking forward in an anxious sort of way to her first meetings with her classes and instructors.

She was idly glancing through some textbooks which Esther had left on her table when Nancy Potter came in to ask Rosemary if she would like to take a get-acquainted walk around the campus. Rosemary accepted eagerly, for she had especially liked the vivacious Nancy on sight. Both girls bundled up tightly, pulled wool stocking caps over their ears, and went out into the moonlight.

The campus presented a stark-white picture-postcard appearance with the fluffy snow banked unsullied against the buildings. The snow-laden trees formed huge graceful urns above the shoveled walks. Somewhere in the distance a male glee club was rehearsing. The strains of "Oh, Susannah" drifted melodiously across the moonlit campus. It all seemed so unreal to Rosemary, something she had dreamed of but had never hoped to attain. Her hopes of attending college had died a final death with her father's passing.

The two girls strolled along arm in arm, the snow crackling under their feet, while Nancy pointed out the different buildings. "That's the library," she said, pointing to a two-story stone building ablaze with lights. "Take it from me, Rosemary, you'll be spending plenty of time there. Professor Burton's a perfect fiend on book reports and he's teaching the English section you'll be in. I had him last semester."

"I don't mind, Nancy," Rosemary said, "I love to read." She didn't want to appear a bookworm to her new friend, but she was anxious to get acquainted with the library and all the treasures it must hold. She had long ago exhausted the limited possibilities of Farmingdale's library. Her dad had always said that if Rosemary was missing, she could always be found at the library.

They strolled on past the library and came to another building which bore the sign, "College Infirmary."

"I wonder if we dare stop in and see Cynthia Sanders," Nancy said thoughtfully. She giggled. "Probably she'd rather we didn't, though, if she had her druthers."

"Why, Nancy?" Rosemary asked, puzzled. She remembered that Cynthia was the one Lawrence girl she hadn't met.

"Cynthia's definitely anti-social," Nancy explained. "I don't think she's volunteered a hundred words in the time I've roomed with her. You'll see when you meet her." She wheeled and tugged at Rosemary's arm. "Come on, let's go in for a lark."

Rosemary was eager to meet the tenth Lawrence girl so they entered the antiseptically clean hall. Nancy spoke to the nurse in charge, who said it would be permissible for them to visit Cynthia for a few minutes.

They walked on down the hall, their rubber heels swishing on the asphalt floor, to a ward that contained four beds. Only two of them were occupied. Nancy approached the bed in the corner where a girl was lying with her eyes closed.

"Cynthia?" she said softly. When the girl did not open her eyes, Nancy repeated it more loudly.

Cynthia's eyes popped open. When she saw the two girls, she instantly assumed a closed, withdrawn expression. Rosemary thought she might have been pretty if she had not looked so on the defensive. Cynthia had lovely blue eyes and an elfin face, but there was no hint of a welcoming smile about her pale lips.

"Oh, hello, Nancy," she said dully, pulling herself up in bed. She gave the impression they weren't exactly welcome.

"Hi, Cynthia. How are you feeling?" Nancy asked brightly.

"Okay, I guess," she replied unconvincingly. Cynthia stared blankly at Rosemary, who was hovering behind Nancy, not knowing just what to do.

Nancy pulled Rosemary forward and made the introductions. Rosemary smiled at Cynthia, but there was no answering smile. Cynthia's lips had a downward cast, and it appeared as though she had not bothered to comb her hair for several days.

"When are you going to get out of this antiseptic prison?" Nancy asked, busily plumping up the pillows behind Cynthia's head and straightening her covers.

"I don't know, Nancy," Cynthia replied, looking annoyed at Nancy's well-meant ministrations. "I'm getting tired of lying here, though." Her voice was pettish. "There's nothing at all to do. I'm bored to death."

"We miss you at the house," Nancy said. "It's lonesome in our little domicile without you." She looked at Rosemary, as though some verbal assistance would be much appreciated.

Cynthia made no reply to Nancy's compliment. Rosemary tried to think of something to say to fill the awkward gap. "Are you a freshman, too, Cynthia?" she asked.

Cynthia shook her head. "Sophomore." Her mouth closed tightly again. There was a long silence in which Cynthia stared at her folded hands on the blanket. Then she laid her head back on the pillow.

"Guess we'd better be running along, Cynthia," Nancy said finally, nudging Rosemary. "The nurse said to stay only a few minutes." She added teasingly, "Now you quit taking it easy and get back on your feet soon, young lady."

Cynthia said shortly, "I'm not pretending I'm sick, if that's what you mean, Nancy." Two red spots appeared high on her cheekbones.

Nancy rolled her eyes toward Rosemary. "Good grief, I was just kidding, Cynthia. Don't take everything so literally. Well, good night."

Rosemary echoed, "Yes, good night, Cynthia. I hope you're better soon."

Cynthia murmured, "Good night," and they hurried out into the hall. They nodded at the nurse as they went past her. When they got outside, Nancy said, "See what I mean, Rosemary? Isn't she weird?"

Rosemary had to agree that Cynthia was difficult, to say the least. "I wonder why she acts so strangely," she said, thinking aloud. She kicked absently at an enormous snowball that someone had left on the path. It smashed and left the toe of her boot white.

Nancy shook her head in bewilderment. "I honestly don't know, Rosemary. Cynthia never talks about her family or clothes or boys or anything other girls talk about. She just goes to classes, comes home, studies, and goes to bed. I can't figure her out at all."

Rosemary thought more about Cynthia as she and Nancy toured the remainder of the campus. There must be a story behind the girl's obvious unhappiness, she decided. Rosemary wished she knew what it was, for she felt a strange kinship with Cynthia. She did not have the bright, poised assurance that some of the other girls had, the quality that Rosemary had always envied in other girls. Yes, she and Cynthia must have a lot in common, she reflected.

Nancy and Rosemary were both beginning to tingle from the cold, so they hurried back to the house. "It's been fun," Rosemary said rather shyly. "Thanks a lot for showing me around, Nancy. Now I'll know where my classes are tomorrow."

"Think nothing of it," Nancy said airily. "Just a Good Deed Gertie, that's me!" They both were giggling like grammar-school girls when they went upstairs to their rooms.

But after Rosemary got into bed and lay staring into the darkness, the glow of good comradeship she had felt with Nancy faded. She thought guiltily of her mother alone in the old house that needed repairs so badly; of her father, gay, fun-loving Phil Rossiter who had never saved for a rainy day.

Why was it that nothing ever worked out right for her? Her dad, whom she had adored, dead at thirty-eight—her mother, having to slave six days a week in a department-store office. She herself never distinguished in anything—not very popular, never quite at ease socially—not an especially good student. She wouldn't even be here at Waverly if Uncle Leon and Aunt Caroline, without children of their own, hadn't offered to pay her way for the first semester.

Rosemary remembered the novel she had read in high school, *Quo Vadis?* That title certainly fit her. "Whither Do You Go?"

On that uncertain note Rosemary finally fell asleep, her damp handkerchief a tight ball in her hand and her eyelids swollen with the tears she had quietly shed into her pillow so Esther would not hear her.

CHAPTER 3

Kitchen Boy

THE NEXT MORNING ROSEMARY PUT ON HER RED SWEATER with the white angora neckline and her navy-blue skirt, telling herself she had to look her best for the first day. First impressions were important. She only wished her lagging spirits were as bright as her red sweater.

Esther came in from the washroom as Rosemary was combing her hair. "You look real cute, Rosemary," she said, dropping her bedroom slippers with a clatter. "That red is pretty with your brown eyes and hair."

Rosemary flushed with unexpected pleasure and murmured a shy thank you. She began feeling better already. Esther took out a smart blue wool suit and stared at it distastefully.

"Guess I'll put this rag on," she said. "Don't you get sick of the same old things after awhile?"

Rosemary nodded. "I'll say. Especially when you don't have many changes to start with." That "old rag" of Esther's was better looking than anything Rosemary owned. Then she told herself how grateful she should be even getting to go to college, without selfishly wishing for a glamorous wardrobe to boot. Sometimes she despised herself for being so self-centered, for always yearning for the things she couldn't afford.

Rosemary took one last critical look at herself in the mirror. "I guess I'd better go, Esther. My first class is clear across the campus." As she took her purse out of her dresser, Rosemary recalled the ten dollars her mother had told her to keep for spending money.

"Would it be all right to leave this extra money in my dresser?" she asked Esther, taking the ten-dollar bill out of her wallet.

Esther frowned and said doubtfully, "I don't believe I would, Rosemary, if I were you." She paused as though trying to decide whether or not she should continue. "Didn't Alicia say anything . . . well . . . about the robberies to you?"

"Robberies?" Rosemary echoed, staring at Esther. "Alicia didn't mention any robberies. Here in the house, you mean?"

Esther nodded. "I suppose Mr. Lawrence wants to soft-pedal it and you can't blame him. It's pretty embarrassing for him, when there's never been any scandal about this house in thirty-five years." She leaned forward, looking like a little girl in her pink slip. "Somebody took an expensive pen and pencil set out of Beverly's room the day before Christmas vacation—one she'd bought for her father's Christmas. Then the day after we came back from vacation, fifty dollars disappeared out of Lee Ann's purse!"

Rosemary looked aghast. "Do you honestly think it was someone here in the house, Esther?"

Esther shrugged. She leaned over and put on a pair of brown loafers. "Nobody seems to know, Rosemary. Mr. Lawrence called the sheriff, though. He came out and

24

looked around but didn't find anything." Her eyes were serious and round. "Yet it's awfully strange. Beverly had showed that pen and pencil set to us just the day before it was stolen. And all the girls know that Lee Ann's mother sends her a lot of money. She mentioned at lunch that day that she had gotten the money late from her mother for a dress and was going downtown that afternoon to buy it. When Lee Ann looked in her purse a couple of hours later, the money was gone." Esther shivered at the recollection.

"It does seem peculiar, doesn't it?" Rosemary said, beginning to gather up her notebooks and pencils. "But surely none of the girls would steal."

Esther looked unconvinced. "You'd better leave your extra money with Mr. Lawrence anyway, Rosemary. He has a safe."

Rosemary put on her coat and went to the door. "Thanks for warning me, Esther. I'll see you later." She lingered uncertainly at the door. "I'm kind of nervous about my first day," she confessed. Esther was just pulling the blue skirt over her head. She began talking before her head emerged.

"I know how you feel, Rosemary, but just act blasé, as though you'd been here all year. Just hold your head up and outstare everybody. Give everyone a big smile."

Rosemary laughed and flicked her hand in farewell. She liked Esther, for she had a lighthearted way about her that pepped you up. Rosemary hurried downstairs, left her money with Mr. Lawrence; and went out into the icy sunshine. Waverly College, here I come, she thought, and joined the other students hurrying across the campus. When anyone looked at her, she smiled right back as Esther had advised.

Since Rosemary was the only first-semester freshman at Lawrence House, she found that she was not in classes with any of the other Lawrence girls. However, she and Esther and Nancy began walking back and forth to classes together and meeting for cokes at Howley's, the campus hangout.

Howley's was a low, one-story wooden building that had been the original college restaurant. Now the college had a gleaming modern cafeteria and Howley's had become "the" spot for music, snacks, and gossip. It was dingy and old-fashioned, but, as Nancy said, it had "simply oodles of atmosphere." The ceiling was made of huge hand-hewn oak beams. A vast stone fireplace at one end always held a blazing fire during the winter months. The choice seats were near the fireplace and were usually grabbed by the upperclassmen.

On Friday afternoon the three girls were having a coke at Howley's when Esther murmured cattily, "Look who just came in, gals. Miss Waverly herself."

Nancy and Rosemary glanced up and saw Beverly Coleman entering with a tall, good-looking chap who had an engaging grin and an unruly cowlick.

Nancy sighed. "Wouldn't you know Beverly would cabbage on to him?" Her tone was one of disgust. Beverly was not at all popular with the other girls, Rosemary had discovered, confirming her own unfavorable first impression of the older girl. The only girl who had a kind word for her was her roommate, Alicia, and, as Esther put it, Alicia as house president had to be impartial and friendly with everyone.

"Who is he?" Rosemary asked, watching the couple. The boy was hovering over Beverly, helping her off with her wrap, while she looked alluringly at him over her shoulder. She had pretended not to see the three younger girls, but Rosemary had the feeling Beverly knew well enough they were watching her.

Rosemary felt a twinge of particularly green envy. Beverly was wearing one of her striking outfits, a hand-knit sweater and skirt of soft coral which was startling with her black hair and ivory skin. There's no doubt about it, Rosemary thought, trying to be fair, Beverly's really a stunning girl.

"That's just Thaddeus Thompson the Third," Nancy breathed soulfully. "Isn't he simply divine, gals? And scads of money besides all the looks and brains."

"They do make a good-looking couple," Rosemary agreed. Beverly's clear-cut profile was etched strikingly against the fire. She looks like the head on a Grecian coin, Rosemary thought. What boy could resist her?

"That's a B.M.O.C., Rosemary," Esther commented, sucking loudly on her straw.

"What's that, Esther?" Rosemary asked. It was hard to learn all the campus lingo at once, but she was determined to be in the know.

"Big Man on the Campus, stupid," Nancy explained.

"Are they going steady?" Rosemary asked, ignoring Nancy.

"According to Beverly they are," Esther said with scorn. "But Thad dated Alicia all last semester. Beverly only started making a play for him lately."

Nancy's eyes twinkled. "That makes for pleasant com-

plications," she said wryly. "Alicia and Beverly being roommates. Look out for fireworks in that direction."

"I'd bet on Beverly in a showdown," Esther said. "Alicia's
too nice to fight over a man. Beverly has that come-thither
look, but definitely!"

In a few moments the three girls finished their cokes and
left. Esther had a late class and Nancy had a library report
to look up, so Rosemary walked back to Lawrence House
alone. She was anxious to see if there would be a letter from
her mother today. She had received only one letter since she
arrived. I wish I had the bus fare to go home this weekend,
she thought, but it was out of the question. It's terrible to
be poor and never to have the money for anything you want
to do, she told herself.

So Rosemary's heart lifted when she saw the familiar
writing on the envelope in her mailbox. She sat down in
the lounge and opened the letter eagerly. The words made
her mother seem close, as though she were there in the
room speaking.

> Dear Rosemary,
>
> So you are getting settled and like your classes and
> Lawrence House. It's nice that you have such an agree-
> able roommate, too. I enjoyed your descriptions of the
> girls and of Mr. Lawrence. I can picture them all. You
> really do have the knack of picturing people. Did you
> know that, my dear?
>
> Since my evenings are free now, I decided to enroll
> in an adult-education class at the high school. I'm
> studying sewing, believe it or not. Classes are three
> nights a week and I've already begun a simple little

blouse for you. You can be expecting some handmade clothes before long.

Jesse Fisher, a new math teacher at the high school, drove me home last night. He's an interesting man, a widower who boards down the street. We got into conversation the first night I enrolled. So you see your old ma is getting along all right, although I do miss you terribly around the house when I come home from work.

Write soon, dear, and enjoy every minute of your precious time in college.

Your loving mother.

Rosemary smiled to herself as she read the letter. A heavy weight lifted from her heart, for she couldn't help feeling guilty about leaving her mother alone. She was honestly glad to hear about Mr. Fisher's interest. It was the best thing for her mother. There had been a long time after her husband's untimely death that Frances Rossiter had moped around and not wanted to meet anyone. There's no earthly reason why Mother shouldn't have men friends, Rosemary told herself, although there was a pang in the region of her heart remembering her parents' devoted love for each other. But Phil Rossiter would not want his beloved wife to be lonely and unhappy. He had been too sociable and warmhearted himself to want his wife to spend the rest of her life grieving for him.

When Rosemary looked up from her letter, feeling peaceful and happy, she noticed Cynthia sitting alone in the corner of the room. She had returned to Lawrence House from the infirmary on Thursday, but Rosemary had not had an opportunity to talk with her. Now Cynthia sat hunched over, staring at a book, but it was obvious that she was not reading.

On impulse, Rosemary walked across the room to her. She spoke cordially. "Hello, Cynthia. I'm glad to see you're up and about again."

Cynthia looked up blindly. Why, she looks as though she's been crying, Rosemary thought. "Uh . . . thanks, Rosemary," she said.

Rosemary glanced around. There was no one else in the lounge at the moment. She sat down beside Cynthia. "Is something wrong, Cynthia?" she asked softly. "I'd like to help if I could."

The girl glanced at Rosemary suspiciously and then dropped her eyes. "Wrong? Why, what makes you ask that, Rosemary?" she replied.

"Oh, intuition, mostly," Rosemary replied, making her voice gentle. "I know how it is to have something on your mind," she said, looking off into space and speaking thoughtfully. "I remember how it was after my father died. I thought I simply couldn't bear it, but now I can think of it without hurting so terribly." She was trying hard to establish rapport with the obviously unhappy girl.

"I'd as well have my father dead, as . . ." Cynthia's voice trailed away, and she swallowed.

"As what?" Rosemary prompted. "Is something wrong at home, Cynthia? Please understand, I'm not trying to pry," she added hastily. "I'd just like to be friends with you." She studied Cynthia's averted profile. It was too bad she always looked so unhappy, because she was pretty and wore becoming clothes.

Cynthia jumped up. "I'm sorry, Rosemary. Excuse me,

please. I've got to go upstairs." She fled from the room. But in her haste she had dropped a newspaper clipping from her book. It fluttered to the floor and lay under a chair.

Rosemary looked at it for a moment and then she picked it up. Although she felt as though she were being nosy, she couldn't resist reading it. It was dated September 15 of the preceding autumn. There was only one paragraph underneath the photograph of an attractive young woman.

MISS RHEA PHILLIPS WEDS CYRUS SANDERS

Cyrus Sanders, well-known local attorney, forty-eight, and Miss Rhea Phillips, twenty-three, were joined in matrimony today at the Town Hall. Miss Phillips was formerly Mr. Sanders' private secretary. Mr. Sanders is a member of a socially prominent family. His only daughter Cynthia is a sophomore at Waverly College. The couple will reside in the Sanders' family home on Boulevard Place, Spencer.

So that's it, Rosemary thought. She pondered a moment over what she could do to help Cynthia. Then she hurried upstairs and knocked briskly on Cynthia's door.

"Come in," Cynthia said in a wan voice. When Rosemary entered, she was lying prone on her bed. She sat up when she saw Rosemary, sighing wearily, as though it were an effort even to be sociable.

"You dropped this out of your book, Cynthia," Rosemary said, handing her the clipping. "I couldn't help reading what it said," she added honestly.

Cynthia snatched the clipping from her and dropped it in her table drawer as though it had burned her fingers. She turned her head away and stared doggedly at the window, but Rosemary saw her chin quiver.

Rosemary sat down on the bed and put her arm around Cynthia's shoulder. "Don't you like your stepmother, Cynthia?" she asked gently.

For a moment there was silence, and then Cynthia blurted out, "It isn't that I don't like her. It's that Rhea doesn't want me around. It's too embarrassing having a stepdaughter almost as old as she is. Can't you see how it is, Rosemary?" Her eyes begged for understanding.

"Yes, I do see, Cynthia," Rosemary said sympathetically.

The dam had broken, for Cynthia began to talk rapidly, as though she were anxious to get something galling out of her system, as though it had been on the tip of her tongue for a long time.

"I knew Rhea before Dad married her, Rosemary. I even liked her. She was a good secretary. But I never dreamed she'd marry Dad!" Cynthia got up and went to the window. Her thin shoulders were rigid. "I've only been home once since they got married, at Christmas. It was simply awful. I don't think my dad even wants me around any more." She turned around, her face white and strained. "He acts so silly with her. Honestly, it's embarrassing, Rosemary. I'm just in the way. I know I am! He never comes to see me at school. He didn't even come when I was sick." Cynthia flopped on her bed again and stared at her feet dejectedly.

Rosemary said nothing for a moment, thinking about the situation, trying to look at it objectively. "Did you let your dad know you were ill, Cynthia?"

"Well, not exactly, Rosemary," Cynthia replied, on the defensive now. "But I didn't write the second week I was in the infirmary. They should have known something was wrong. You'd think they'd at least call up to find out if I was sick." Her voice rang with bitterness and rejection.

Rosemary was at a loss to know what to say further, so she merely patted Cynthia's shoulder. "I can certainly see why you're upset, Cynthia," she said. "But perhaps you haven't really given your stepmother a chance. She probably feels as awkward as you do."

At that moment the dinner bell chimed. Rosemary stood up, secretly relieved at the interruption. "You'd better wipe your eyes, Cynthia," she suggested. "You'll feel better now you've told someone. You really should get closer to Nancy. She's a swell girl."

Cynthia nodded. "I know she is, Rosemary. But I don't like to bore other people with my problems. I don't know why I spilled so much to you, except I was so down in the dumps today. Nancy's always so jolly, she's probably sick of having me for a roommate."

Rosemary thought rather uncharitably that Cynthia was more nearly right than she realized. Nancy had confided to Rosemary that Cynthia was getting on her nerves with her eternal melancholy.

Together they went down to supper. If the other girls noticed Cynthia's swollen eyes, everyone tactfully avoided mentioning the fact. Nancy was especially gay. Soon she had everyone laughing with her imitation of her physical cd teacher who had taught gymnastics in a reform school and was using the same methods at Waverly with disastrous results.

After supper, when the opportunity arose, Rosemary drew Alicia aside and told her briefly about Cynthia's personal problem. "You're from the same town, aren't you, Alicia?" she asked, pursuing an idea that had come to her at the table while Nancy was holding forth.

"Yes, I am, Rosemary. Why? Did you have something in mind?"

"Well, it's only a suggestion, Alicia," she said modestly. "I'm really concerned about Cynthia. She's terribly despondent. Perhaps you might talk to Mr. Sanders. He and his wife probably don't even realize how left out of their lives Cynthia feels."

"That's a good idea, Rosemary," Alicia said, looking at her with dawning respect. She entered quickly into the spirit of the plan. "Mr. Sanders attends the same church as my folks. I'll make it a point next weekend to have a talk with him." She added, "I've tried hard myself to make friends with Cynthia, but she's frozen me out, as she has everyone else in the house. I'm glad she finally confided in you, Rosemary. You can be sure I'll not pass what you told me any further."

Rosemary felt proud that she had accomplished something with Cynthia that no one else in the house had been able to do. Of all the girls, why had Cynthia chosen her to confide in? Rosemary didn't know the answer, but she felt that she had made one friend, at least.

She went out to the dining room for a glass of water and found that the table had already been cleared. She heard a loud off-key whistling in the kitchen. It certainly wasn't Nellie, the colored housekeeper, who was addicted to Negro spirituals in spite of Mr. Lawrence's remonstrances. Rosemary was curious enough to peek through a crack in the swinging door to see who was in the kitchen.

A strange boy was swinging dishes from the sink to the drainboard in a fast motion to the rhythm of "Buckle Down, Winsocki." He wore a voluminous white apron and his shirt sleeves were rolled up above his elbows. Nellie was drying the dishes and chuckling at the boy's speedy methods. She turned and caught Rosemary looking in the door.

"Hello, Miss Rossiter," she said. "Did you want somethin', honey?"

Rosemary was covered with confusion at being caught. "Not exactly, Nellie," she said weakly. "I was ... looking for Mr. Lawrence."

"He ain't out here," Nellie replied. "I ain't seen him since supper. I think he went out."

The boy had glanced over his shoulder. As he did so, a dish slipped from his wet hands and crashed on the tile floor. He looked down ruefully. "Oh, boy, first day on the job and I have to break a dish! Wouldn't you know it?" He grinned at Rosemary, got the broom and dustpan, and cheerfully began sweeping up the debris, still whistling.

He isn't a very good-looking boy, Rosemary decided, rather ordinary, in fact, but he has a nice friendly smile, a well-shaped head with close-set ears, and twinkling gray eyes. She was trying to decide how to retreat gracefully when Nellie came to her rescue.

"This here is Gray Horton, Miss Rossiter. He come to help out in the kitchen the rest of the semester."

There was a sly twinkle in Gray's eyes as he bowed low, holding out the apron comically, and said with exaggerated formality, "I'm indeed honored to make your acquaintance,

Miss Rosemary Rossiter. I'm in your public-speaking class but I don't suppose you've deigned to notice me."

Rosemary smiled with some embarrassment, for it was true that she hadn't noticed him. He wasn't a boy who would stand out in a group. But she evaded his comment by saying, "I like that class, don't you? Especially Professor Hayworth."

Gray was back washing the dishes in a steady rhythm. He replied over his shoulder, "It's a good class, even if I am a dud at public speaking. Professor Hayworth is a good egg, all right."

Rosemary felt it was time to make an exit, so she said, "Good night, Nellie. I'll be seeing you in class, Gray."

"You can be sure of that, Rosemary," he returned, with another bow. She left, feeling faintly foolish, wondering just what he had meant by that.

When she reached her room, Rosemary looked in her mirror. Her eyes were shining and she looked almost pretty for once. Gray Horton was the first boy who had shown the slightest interest in her since she had arrived at Waverly. But she mustn't read something into his tone he probably hadn't even meant, she told herself severely. He probably had only meant he'd be seeing her in public-speaking class. Oh, well, she could dream, couldn't she?

CHAPTER 4

The Speech Clinic

ON FRIDAY AFTERNOON OF HER SECOND WEEK AT WAVERLY, Rosemary drifted downstairs and found Fern sitting in the hall, looking as perturbed as usual. Why did the girl always make her want to laugh when she was so deadly serious, Rosemary asked herself.

"Hi, Fern," she said sweetly. "Waiting for someone?"

Fern sighed. "Wilma, of course. Honestly, Rosemary, that girl has no sense of time at all. She promised to meet me at two thirty to go to the library. Here it is three and she hasn't shown up yet." Fern was wearing another of what Rosemary always called to herself Fern's Puritan dresses, only this one was dark blue instead of gray.

Rosemary decided that this was a good opportunity to become better acquainted with Fern, whom she had talked to only briefly, so she sat down beside her. "You girls don't see exactly eye to eye, do you?" she commented, giving Fern an opening. She seemed to want a chance to talk, especially about Wilma.

"We're nothing alike, if that's what you mean," Fern said, picking up the bait. "All Wilma thinks about is boys and having fun, and I .... Well, I've always been more serious-minded, you might say." She smiled primly with

37

her pale lips pressed together. "But we get along all right, Rosemary. Wilma doesn't bother my things and I don't bother hers. At least, we don't have the problem of trading clothes the way some roommates do." She glanced suspiciously at Rosemary's sweater as though she suspected it might be Esther's.

Rosemary was smiling inwardly at the vision of the two girls in each other's widely dissimilar clothes. Fern lowered her voice confidentially. "Did you know that Wilma was late so many times last semester that Mr. Lawrence only let her back in the house this semester on probation? If she has any more infringements, she'll have to leave at the midterm period." She blinked her scanty eyelashes rapidly.

"Indeed," Rosemary murmured. She wondered if Fern didn't find some ulterior satisfaction in Wilma's state of disgrace.

"I'm trying my very best to help Wilma with her studies," Fern announced virtuously. "Fortunately, we're both majoring in history. Wilma's just on the border line, though. I'd really hate to see her flunk out, although I must say it would be her own fault. She isn't stupid; she just doesn't care."

At that moment Wilma came rushing in the front door, panting as usual. "I'm sorry, Fern, truly I am. It was just one of those things," she said vaguely, smiling at Rosemary. "Hope you haven't been waiting long."

Rosemary smiled back. There was something exceedingly likable about Wilma even if she was a scatterbrain and overly boy conscious. "Do you ever just walk, Wilma?" she asked teasingly. "I've never seen you that you weren't on the run."

The other girl laughed good-naturedly. "Hardly ever," she said. "The trouble is—I just can't keep my dates straight." She took hold of Fern's arm and pulled her up. "Come on, Fernie, if I don't get that report for history, you know what'll happen." She didn't sound in the least worried, though, Rosemary noted.

Fern clucked like a mother hen with one chick. "Honestly, Wilma, will you ever learn?" She looked at Rosemary as though seeking corroboration. Rosemary smiled noncommittally, not wanting to take sides.

The two girls left the house arm in arm. Rosemary, smiling to herself, watched them go off down the walk. Fern was evidently giving Wilma a stiff lecture and Wilma was nodding and looking properly contrite. Fern would miss Wilma if she did flunk out, Rosemary thought, with sudden clear insight, for then she wouldn't have anyone to mother and scold. Fern would be lost without her irresponsible roommate. Some people just weren't happy unless they had someone to hover over and complain about and Fern was of that type.

Rosemary turned to go upstairs, trying to decide what she should do the rest of the afternoon, when she met Alicia coming down, dressed, as usual, in a smart suit that set off her tall, slender blondness to advantage. Her camel's-hair coat swung from her shoulders.

"At loose ends, Rosemary?" Alicia asked.

"Yes, Alicia," Rosemary replied lazily. "I've lots to do, but can't get started on anything in particular."

"Want to walk over to the speech department with me?" Alicia asked.

Rosemary eagerly seized the opportunity, for speech was

already turning out to be her favorite subject and Professor Hayworth her favorite teacher. "Wait until I get my coat and I'll be right with you, Alicia," she said.

They walked across the campus, which was quiet and practically deserted now in late afternoon. Most students left the campus for the weekend unless there were games or special activities planned. The sun was just slanting over the library roof, casting long, interesting shadows on the snow. Rosemary loved this time of day just before dusk. It always made her pensive and gave her poetic inspirations —if she could only get them down into words. But her feeble attempts at writing poetry had ended in failure.

"I didn't know you took speech, Alicia," she said, breaking their companionable silence. She liked the older girl, who was so much friendlier than her roommate Beverly, who deliberately ignored the freshman girls.

"You didn't? I'm a speech major, Rosemary," Alicia replied, with pride in her voice. "I'm especially interested in speech correction. In fact, I've been tutoring a little boy every Tuesday and Friday afternoon since Christmas."

"That sounds awfully interesting," Rosemary said, looking at her companion with admiration. "I'm afraid I know nothing at all about speech correction. Something new, isn't it?"

Alicia smiled. "Not exactly new, Rosemary, but it's just coming into its own, you might say. A lot of grammar schools are hiring speech correctionists now, because so many children have speech defects."

"Are they all physical defects, Alicia? I'd think you'd have to have medical training to handle that kind."

"You do have to have some training in biology and the

anatomy of the human body," Alicia replied. "But some speech defects are from emotional causes. Stammering, for instance, can be caused by trying to make a naturally left-handed child write right-handed. Or a child can have an inferiority complex, or he can have other emotional disturbances which might upset his speech, like those caused by a broken home or a death in the family."

Like me, Rosemary thought. It's a wonder I didn't stammer after my dad died. But maybe I was too old to start stammering, being rather vague about the subject.

They had come to the statue of Samuel Waverly, the school's founder. Some jokester had put a school pennant in his iron hand. When they walked by the library, Gray Horton was just trotting down the steps. He waved at the girls and Rosemary waved back, feeling her cheeks flush. Gray went off in the opposite direction and Alicia looked at her with a little knowing smile.

They reached the speech department, which was on the first floor of the Liberal Arts Building, and entered a glass-walled room that Rosemary hadn't seen before.

"This is the speech clinic, Rosemary," Alicia said. It looked like a regular doctor's office, Rosemary thought, all white and steel and medical looking. She was interested to see the recording and testing apparatus on the steel tables. Reading charts hung on the walls. She recognized a wire recorder and what she assumed to be line drawings of the vocal apparatus.

Alicia whispered. "There's my little student outside. His mother brings him and returns for him. Professor Hayworth feels that is best, because parents can be disturbing sometimes. They don't mean to be, but they are."

Rosemary looked through the glass. A small boy was swinging his legs on the bench in the waiting room. He was looking at a magazine with absorption, although he had it turned upside down.

"He's cute, isn't he?" Rosemary said, captivated by the attractive child.

"Yes, he is perfectly darling, Rosemary," Alicia agreed. "Michael's five years old, but he's never learned to pronounce his consonants. Professor Hayworth examined him and found nothing wrong with his speech apparatus. Michael was sick a lot during infancy and his parents babied him. He could just point and get what he wanted. Now, since he's going to school next fall, he must learn to talk. His parents are getting concerned about him." She opened the door. "Come in, Michael," she called.

The little boy trotted in, looking about him with inquisitive eyes. Alicia knelt beside him and took off his coat. He kissed her on the cheek. "Hel-lo, Teach-er," he enunciated carefully. He stared curiously at Rosemary.

"How are you today, Michael?" Alicia asked, looking down at him affectionately.

"Okay, Teacher," he said clearly. Then he smiled and pointed to his feet. "I aa oo ees," he said, lapsing into baby talk. Both girls looked down in puzzlement and saw the shiny new shoes he was pointing at so proudly.

Alicia set him up on a chair. "Now, Michael, it's 'I have new shoes.' Won't you try to say it correctly for me?"

He tried manfully to imitate the sounds by making wide grimaces. But the correct sounds wouldn't come out. He kept glancing toward Rosemary.

"Perhaps you'd better wait outside," Alicia suggested

quietly to Rosemary. "Michael's rather shy, I've found." She whispered, "I'll leave the door slightly ajar so you can hear if you want to stick around."

Rosemary wouldn't have left for anything. This was going to be quite interesting. From the waiting room she watched while Alicia put the boy through a series of simple exercises to limber up his jaws, mouth, and tongue. Alicia pronounced each consonant sound, then, and patiently showed Michael where to place his tongue to reproduce the sound. She held a mirror for him so he could see his own tongue. Then she combined each consonant with a simple word, going over and over each word until Michael had mastered it.

After that they rested a few minutes and Alicia gave Michael a candy bar. After he had gotten a drink of water and settled down again, Alicia began reciting simple nursery rhymes, which Michael struggled to repeat after her. Some of his words were clear; others were a mere jumble of sounds.

It was obvious that the child adored Alicia, for he tried valiantly to please her. Rosemary marveled at Alicia's patience. She had always seemed so crisp and businesslike at the house, but here she betrayed a gentleness that made her more endearing.

What a worth-while profession, Rosemary thought, helping children to learn to speak clearly. What a difference it should make in their future lives.

The lesson lasted for forty-five minutes. At the end of that time Michael's mother returned for him. She was a fine-looking young woman who talked earnestly with Alicia about her son's progress. Michael put on his coat himself and kissed Alicia again. He said clearly, "Good-by, Teacher."

Rosemary smiled at him and his mother as they passed

through the waiting room. "That's all a little tyke can take without getting restless," Alicia said as soon as they were out of earshot. "If I could only see Michael every day instead of twice a week I could really accomplish a great deal more. Still, he's making some progress." She put on her coat.

"Can his parents help at all, Alicia?" Rosemary asked.

"I give his mother rhymes to practice with him. But, oddly enough, a child responds better to a stranger than to his own parents. Michael's quite proud of having a teacher all his own, you see. His mother says he brags about it to all his playmates." The girls smiled at each other.

"I'm so glad you asked me to come, Alicia," Rosemary said, rising. "I wasn't even aware that Waverly had a speech clinic."

"A lot of colleges have speech clinics now," Alicia said, as she turned off the lights and locked the doors. "And they're free to anyone who wishes to take advantage of them. But there's such a shortage of trained speech correctionists, Rosemary. Many children never have the chance to get help until it's too late. Professor Hayworth was the one who got me interested in this work. He's a whiz at it."

They walked down the deserted corridor, their heels clicking in the silence. "It's dead around here on Friday afternoons, isn't it?" Alicia commented as they went outside into the lavender dusk. "I'm going home myself tomorrow."

Rosemary felt a sharp pang of the first real homesickness she had experienced all week. She had not seen her mother for two weeks now, the longest she had ever been away from her. But so much had happened in those two weeks that she had had little time to be lonely. It was only in moments like this that she thought longingly of her mother and of Farmingdale.

So Rosemary was delighted when her uncle Leon called her that night. He had business in Waverly on Saturday, he said, and would drive her home if she wanted to go. She could surprise her mother, if she wished. He promised to drive Rosemary back to the college on Sunday afternoon. Of course her mother was ecstatic when Rosemary surprised her in the midst of her Saturday cleaning. She had the day off from the store, she said, to make up for overtime she had worked. They talked all day Saturday, went to church Sunday morning, and had dinner at home.

Then Uncle Leon and Aunt Caroline drove Rosemary back to the campus. Her mother had been apologetic about not riding back with her. "I've a date with Mr. Fisher for a concert," she said. "He's already bought the tickets. If I'd only known you were coming, dear." She looked rather embarrassed.

"That's all right, Mother," Rosemary said quickly. "You go ahead and have a good time."

"He's such good company, Rosemary," Frances Rossiter said. Her eyes were pleading for understanding. "I'd almost forgotten what it was like to go out with an attractive man."

"I'm glad for you, Mother," Rosemary assured her mother, dispelling the awkwardness between them. She knew her mother was afraid she might resent her new masculine friendship. "It's good to know you're not sitting here alone all the time. I hope I can meet Mr. Fisher before long."

Her mother looked relieved. She even looked younger, Rosemary decided, the way she had looked when her father was alive. She had her hair arranged a new way and the blue shadows were gone from beneath her eyes. A man's interest could do wonders for a lonely woman. After all, Rosemary's father had been gone for more than a year now. Was it really a whole year? Rosemary thought, shocked at the discovery. A year ago this time I thought I'd never be able to go on without Dad. I hope I'm not being disloyal to him to be glad that Mother has a man friend and I'm beginning to feel interest in things again, too.

CHAPTER 5

An Afternoon at Howley's

WHEN ROSEMARY RETURNED TO LAWRENCE HOUSE ON SUN-day afternoon Esther was not in their room. When Alicia returned to the house later she told Rosemary that Esther had unexpectedly signed out on Saturday afternoon, saying that she was going home to Freesburg for the weekend.

Alicia drew Rosemary aside in the lounge. "I talked with Cynthia's father," she said softly. "You were right, Rosemary. He didn't realize at all how Cynthia felt about things at home. He said he had been thoughtless in his new happiness. He and his wife are coming over to take Cynthia home next weekend. He's going to call Cynthia this week."

"That's wonderful," Rosemary said, glad that her idea had worked out. "I won't say anything to Cynthia about it, Alicia. Let's let her think it was all her father's idea."

Alicia agreed wholeheartedly. Rosemary felt a glow of warm satisfaction. She hoped things worked out for Cynthia now so she would not be so unhappy and lonely.

Rosemary spent the evening working on a book report. By ten o'clock Esther had not returned. She drove her own car and was an excellent driver, but Rosemary couldn't help worrying about her. Finally Rosemary went to bed after having convinced herself that the reliable Esther would have a good excuse for being late.

Sometime later Rosemary was awakened suddenly. She lay utterly quiet for a moment, trying to decide what it was that had awakened her. There was a sharp tap. Rosemary realized, then, that it had been a pebble striking against the windowpane.

She jumped out of bed and ran to the window. The clock in the library tower was just tolling twelve. Rosemary looked down, and, to her surprise, saw Esther looking up at her. Her car was parked at the curb and she was a tiny dark figure silhouetted against the snow. Rosemary lifted the window, making as little noise as possible.

"Rosemary, come down and open the door," Esther called softly. "I'm locked out."

"Just a minute, Esther. I'll be right down." Rosemary put on her robe and slipped out into the hall. Only a night light was burning at the top of the stairs. She paused and listened. The house was completely quiet. She knew she would be penalized along with Esther if she were discovered, but she had to risk it.

Treading softly, Rosemary crept down the carpeted stairway and drew back the bolt with a minimum of noise. Esther slipped inside. Rosemary caught a whiff of fresh tobacco smoke. Esther didn't smoke. Had there been a boy with her before she called up to Rosemary?

The two girls crept up the stairs. Halfway up a step creaked. They both stopped stock-still, every sense alert. Rosemary swallowed. Silence. They hurried on up the stairs and shut the door into their room quietly.

Esther, her face white and drawn, took off her coat and flopped on the bed. "Am I exhausted!" she groaned. She threw her hat toward a chair, kicked off her shoes, and

48

wriggled her toes. "Thanks for letting me in, Rosemary. This is the first time I've been late."

Rosemary got back into bed and lay looking at Esther. There was a tense quality about her roommate that puzzled her. It wasn't like her at all, for Esther was usually so poised and uncomplicated.

"Did you have car trouble?" she asked, trying to sound casual.

Esther started taking things out of her bag. "I just didn't start back early enough, that's all." She didn't look at Rosemary, who had the impression that Esther wasn't being entirely honest.

"How far is it to Freesburg, Esther?" she couldn't resist asking.

"Oh, about eighty-five miles," Esther said, pulling her dress over her head. Her voice was muffled. "Driving was bad tonight. The road was slippery in spots. Did Mr. Lawrence know I was late?"

"I don't know," Rosemary replied. "Of course, Alicia knew you weren't back at ten but maybe she didn't report you, since it's your first time."

"I hope not," Esther murmured. She put on her pajamas and yawned. "I'll be dead tomorrow. Wouldn't you know I'd have an eight o'clock? Good night, Rosemary."

She turned out the light and climbed into bed. Rosemary lay in the dark thinking. There was something Esther hadn't told her, she was sure of that. She had had a withdrawn, reserved quality tonight that was unlike her.

Rosemary fell asleep again finally. Toward dawn she was awakened again, this time by a moaning sound. She sat up in bed and listened. It was Esther threshing about in her bed.

49

Rosemary got up and went over to her roommate's bed. She switched on her bed lamp. Esther looked ill. She opened her eyes and looked up at Rosemary.

"What's the matter, Esther?" Rosemary asked, frightened by her roommate's strange appearance.

"I'm sick at my stomach, Rosemary," Esther moaned.

"Should I call Alicia?"

"No use . . . getting her out of bed. Have you got an aspirin?"

Rosemary remembered the bottle her mother had put in her suitcase. She got two pills and a glass of water and gave them to Esther. "I still think I ought to call someone," she said. "You look terrible."

"No, I don't want you to, Rosemary," Esther said sharply. "I'll be all right. Too much weekend. I ate too much. Go back to bed."

Rosemary got back into bed and listened to her room-mate's tossing and turning. In a little while she seemed calmer, and still later Rosemary heard her deep breathing. Rosemary turned over and punched her pillow. This has been some night! she thought. I'm glad I don't have a class until nine tomorrow. I'd never be able to get up otherwise.

But, surprisingly enough, Esther was her usual bright self in the morning. She dismissed her illness of the night lightly. "Probably just nerves," she said casually. "I was nervous about getting back late and my stomach always churns when I'm tense."

At breakfast Rosemary thought she saw Mr. Lawrence looking at her and Esther in a speculative fashion over his glasses. She pretended not to notice and nibbled away non-chalantly at her toast. Had he heard her slipping downstairs last night to let Esther in? She was starting her third week in the house and hadn't had any demerits yet. But was her luck going to hold out?

She knew the worst when Alicia found her and Esther in their room after breakfast. "I'm sorry to have bad news for you gals," she said. "Mr. Lawrence heard you letting Esther in last night, Rosemary. You're both fined ten demerits."

Esther looked at Rosemary ruefully. "Golly, I'm sorry, Rosemary. I should have rung the bell, and then I wouldn't have gotten you in trouble, too."

"That's all right, Esther," Rosemary said, although she was secretly mortified. "What do ten demerits mean, Alicia?"

"Another five and you're confined to the house for a whole weekend," the house president replied.

"Wouldn't you know old Eagle Ears would hear me come in?" Esther said. "I don't think any girl has ever slipped into this house since I've been here."

Rosemary decided that she was going to be extra careful from now on. It wouldn't be much fun to have to stick in the house a whole weekend when the other girls were out having fun. When she went past Mr. Lawrence's desk on the way to her nine-o'clock class, he said sternly, "I hope you adhere to the house rules in the future, Miss Rossiter."

Rosemary flushed and murmured meekly, "I'll try to, Mr. Lawrence."

That afternoon Rosemary was studying in her room when she heard Mr. Lawrence calling upstairs. "Esther

Mercer, telephone." Rosemary stuck her head out of the door. "Esther's not here, sir. She has a three-o'clock class today." Mr. Lawrence thanked her, and Rosemary had just closed the door when he called upstairs again.

"Miss Rossiter, could you come down? It's Esther's father. He wants to speak with you."

"Certainly, sir." She went downstairs to the telephone in the hall.

"This is Amil Mercer, in Freesburg, Rosemary," a deep voice said. "Esther has written us all about you."

Rosemary murmured something polite. "Will you please deliver Esther a message for her mother and me?" Mr. Mercer continued. "Esther was to come home next weekend, but I've urgent business in California and we're leaving tonight on the plane. Tell her we'll definitely be expecting her the following weekend."

"I certainly shall, sir," Rosemary promised. There was a pause at the other end of the line, and Rosemary heard a feminine voice in the background.

"Just a minute, Rosemary," he said. "Mrs. Mercer wants to speak with you."

A gracious voice spoke then. "Rosemary, I'm glad to meet you even if only by telephone. Esther has written what a pleasant roommate you are."

"Thank you, Mrs. Mercer," Rosemary said, rather flustered. "Esther and I do get along nicely."

"You tell our little girl that we're terribly lonesome to see her," Mrs. Mercer said plaintively. "She hasn't been home since Christmas. I don't understand why she always has to get stuck there on the weekends with her library work." Mrs. Mercer sighed. "I hope she's eating right, too.

I always worry so about her food away from home. Esther's such a baby. She really needs someone to look after her."

Rosemary stammered out something about the food being delicious at Lawrence House. But she was thinking about what Mrs. Mercer had said. Where in the world had Esther been on the weekend if she hadn't gone home?

Rosemary hung up, and returned thoughtfully to her room, still puzzling over Esther's weekend whereabouts. When Esther came in for supper, Rosemary delivered her parents' message without comment, but she closely watched her roommate's reaction. Esther flushed, said, "Thanks, Rosemary," and offered no explanation for the discrepancy in stories. Rosemary was more puzzled than ever, but told herself it was really none of her business and tried to put the matter out of her mind.

The next day Gray caught Rosemary at the door after her history class. "Would you like to go over to Howley's for a coke?" he asked diffidently. "I don't have to be at the house until five."

Rosemary had not talked with Gray since the night Nellie had introduced them in the kitchen. She had noted, though, that his speeches were well delivered and well thought out in public-speaking class. She often felt his eyes on her in class, and his quiet regard always made her pulses throb a little.

"I'd love to, Gray," she said. She liked his straightforward gray eyes and his gentlemanly manners, even though his clothes were old and shabby.

Gray walked her over to Howley's at a fast pace that left

her gasping for breath. "My goodness, Gray, I never saw a boy walk as fast as you do," she finally gasped. "I'm all out of breath."

He shortened his steps. "I didn't realize I was wearing you out. I'm so used to being on the run all the time, I do it even when it isn't necessary. Take a deep breath and let it out easy."

She followed his instructions, and the tight band on her chest relaxed. They entered the smoky room and Gray found them a cozy table in the corner near the fireplace. He helped her off with her coat and hung his own coat on the rack over it. She noted that the lining was ragged, but the coat wore a jaunty, proud air like its owner.

While they were sipping their cokes, Gray looked at her with a roguish gleam in his eyes. "I hope this won't hurt your social standing, Rosemary, being seen in Howley's with the Lawrence House dishwasher."

Rosemary's lips curved. "I'm not a snob, Gray. Anyway, I'm just as poor as anybody on the campus." She decided to be completely honest with Gray. "I couldn't even have come to college if I hadn't had financial help from my uncle. My father didn't leave any insurance."

She remembered that fateful day when Uncle Leon had asked her if she'd like to go to Waverly. They were sitting in the kitchen of her home on Maple Drive, the old house where she had been born.

Uncle Leon, a strong-looking man with a weatherbeaten countenance and the callused hands of a farmer, said, "I'll help you the first semester, Rosemary. Then maybe you can find a job or win a scholarship. I have the idea you'll be able to continue if you once get started."

Rosemary argued that she couldn't leave her mother alone. Uncle Leon said her mother was all in favor of her going.

While she had been thinking over his proposal, Rosemary stood looking out of the kitchen window at the familiar scene, at Mrs. Kelly's littered back yard and the perpetually dingy laundry which blew stiffly in the wind; at Mrs. Kelly's gray cat, Mittens, and her latest brood of ugly, nondescript kittens.

Then Rosemary had looked at their own kitchen as though she had never seen it before: at the yellow dimity curtains, stiffly starched; at the worn place in the linoleum before the sink; at the impossibly bright blue morning-glories in the wallpaper her father had hung. She knew that her mother couldn't bear to replace that paper because it always reminded her of Phil.

Yes, it would be fun to have a change of scenery, she decided, to meet new people and some new boys in particular. So Rosemary had accepted with the stipulation that the money would be a loan, to be paid back when she was self-supporting. . . .

Now Gray was nodding understandingly. "I know what you mean, Rosemary. I couldn't have come to Waverly, either, if I hadn't gotten a part scholarship. My folks couldn't help at all financially. You've seen me in action paying off the rest of my expenses."

They both laughed, and a comfortable silence fell between them while they looked around the room. Rosemary couldn't remember when she had felt so at ease with a boy. She could lay aside all pretenses and just be herself. She

felt under no obligation to be sparkling or pseudo-sophisti-
cated with Gray.

"What are you majoring in, Gray?" she finally asked.

"I want to be a veterinarian," he replied. "I've always
loved animals. Growing up on the farm, I guess. But it's a
long haul, Rosemary."

While Gray was speaking, Rosemary's idle glance around
the room stopped suddenly. Was that Esther sitting in that
dark corner? She peered around a fat boy who was showing
some card tricks to an appreciative group. It was Esther,
sitting with a strange boy. Rosemary had never before seen
Esther with any boy at all. To her knowledge, Esther had
not had a date since they had been rooming together.

Rosemary wondered who the boy was. He was good-
looking in a dark, foreign way and had a thick shock of
shining black hair which needed cutting. They were talking
earnestly and seemed unaware of the confusion around
them. Esther was answering the boy with a good deal of
vivacity. They appeared to be arguing about something in
a friendly manner.

Rosemary brought her wandering attention back to Gray's
last statement. "Yes, any profession is a long haul, Gray,"
she said quickly, afraid he would think she wasn't listening.
"But it's worth the struggle. I haven't made up my mind
yet what I'm going to major in."

Gray rubbed his ear lobe with his right thumb, a gesture
which she found intriguing for some reason. He looked at
her appraisingly for a long moment. "I think you're the
nicest girl at Lawrence House, Rosemary," he said unexpectedly. "Some of those gals, like that Beverly Coleman,

wouldn't be caught dead drinking cokes with the kitchen help."

Rosemary had to agree silently, but she felt she had to reassure Gray. She understood how he felt because she often felt the same way herself. "Not all the girls are like Beverly, Gray," she said. "Esther Mercer, my roommate, is a very nice girl. She's sitting over there in the corner." She pointed Esther out to Gray.

"I know that guy with her," he said. "Tony Risotti his name is. He works in the bookstore." So Rosemary knew the boy's name, at least.

Soon afterward Gray and Rosemary walked slowly back to Lawrence House. It was growing dusk, and a blue haze hung over the campus. The snow had melted, and puddles dotted the paths. Gray guided her around them with a touch on her elbow. "I only wish I had a velvet cloak," he said.

When they reached the front walk they paused, and Gray looked down at her. "Maybe we can do this again soon, Rosemary," he said, taking her hand. She felt the calluses on his palm. "You're the first girl I've even looked at since I've been on the campus," he continued. "I never felt I had the time or the money for girls. Besides, most girls aren't interested in a guy perpetually without funds." He grinned, but his eyes were serious and steady on hers.

Rosemary knew she had to say just the right thing. It was an important moment for both of them. "Let's," she said softly. "I enjoyed being with you very much, Gray." She watched his eyes light up. "I'll be seeing you tomorrow," she said, "in public-speaking class."

Gray watched Rosemary go into the house and then he went around the sidewalk to the kitchen. He was whistling gaily when he entered the back door. He just grinned self-consciously when Nellie, chuckling, said, "That's a mighty sweet little girl you got yourself, kitchen boy. I saw you courtin' her out there."

CHAPTER 6

The Valentine Day Dance

IT WAS THE DAY BEFORE VALENTINE DAY AND THE OCCU-
pants of Lawrence House were abuzz with excitement over
the first social event of the semester, the Valentine Day
Dance. Everyone had been assigned to a committee. Rosemary and Esther were put on the decorating committee.
Alicia, in her position as house president, would supervise
all the arrangements.

Rosemary went upstairs to ask Alicia's advice about some
red crepe paper she and Esther had resurrected from a basement closet. Most of the girls were in the lounge rearrang-
ing the furniture to make space for dancing. Esther was
downstairs cutting crepe-paper curlicues to hang from the
ceiling.

Rosemary started to knock on Alicia's door when she
heard Beverly's voice rising shrilly inside. "Alicia Barnes,
you knew good and well I'd be inviting Thad. You just hurried up and invited him to spite me!"

Rosemary stood still and dropped her raised hand. Perhaps this wasn't exactly the moment to bother Alicia, she
thought. She started to move away quietly, and then heard
Alicia's cool voice replying, "Now, Beverly, I did no such
thing. I just happened to run into Thad the night Mr. Law-

59

rence announced the party. So I invited him. After all, I did date him first, remember."

"So what? You don't own Thad, Alicia, even though you'd like to."

The door burst open and Beverly came storming out. Her usually white face was red and her eyes were shooting sparks. She almost collided with Rosemary, who was embarrassed at being caught eavesdropping.

"Oh, look out! You freshmen are always in the way!" Beverly snapped. She banged into the washroom. Rosemary waited uncertainly, wondering if she ought to go in. Alicia came to the door and saw her standing there. She had a firm set to her chin, but otherwise there was no indication that she had been quarreling with her roommate.

"Come in, Rosemary. I suppose you heard the tail end of that little set-to." She shrugged. "Beverly won't speak to me now until after the dance."

Rosemary patted her arm comfortingly. "I wouldn't care, Alicia. Beverly can find somebody else for the dance, with all the boys she has hanging around her."

Alicia smiled. "But she wanted Thad, Rosemary. Beverly started making a play for Thad after we began rooming together. I think it was just to prove she could take him away from me." Her smile wavered, and Rosemary could see Alicia was not so unperturbed as she pretended to be. "What did you want to see me about?"

Rosemary showed her the red crepe paper. Alicia thought it was too old and faded to use. "By the way, Rosemary," she asked suddenly, as though just thinking of it, "do you have a date for the dance?"

"Yes, Alicia. Gray Horton, the boy who works in the kitchen."

Alicia looked surprised and then pleased. "I'm glad, Rosemary. He's a nice boy. Mr. Lawrence says he's the best kitchen help he's ever had."

Rosemary felt a sense of personal gratification, even though Gray and she were just friends. The older girl's approval meant a lot to her, for she respected Alicia's opinion as she would have an older sister's.

Beverly swished back into the room, her head held high. She pointedly ignored both girls and snatched her fur coat from the closet, then banged the door as she went out.

Rosemary and Alicia smiled at each other. "She'll get over it, eventually," Alicia said. "She always does. Her father has spoiled Beverly so much that she thinks everybody ought to give in to her no matter what the occasion."

Rosemary thought how true that was. Beverly had more beautiful clothes and possessions than anyone else in the house, even more than Lee Ann. At the moment a pile of expensive-looking jewelry was tossed carelessly on her dresser.

The girls had decided they would make the preparations on Thursday, the day before the dance, so they would not be exhausted before the festivities. On Friday evening no one ate much supper because of the breathless anticipation that permeated the house. Even the blasé Beverly looked excited. After supper they all hurried upstairs to get ready, for their dates would be arriving at eight o'clock. The house was spick-and-span, aglow with lights and smelling of the anise-seed cookies that Nellie had baked to serve with the fruit punch.

Rosemary thought Esther looked a little paler than usual. She noticed that Esther had lingered a long time over a letter from home, but finally she stuck it away in her desk and began chattering in her usual vivacious manner while they got dressed.

For the party Esther was wearing a white wool jersey with red belt and a red choker; Rosemary, her green taffeta with the sweetheart neckline and the single strand of pearls her aunt and uncle had given her for Christmas.

"How did you ever meet Tony, Esther?" she asked idly as they applied last-minute nail polish, Esther, scarlet to match her belt, and Rosemary, pink. They were sitting on the sides of their beds.

"He's from my home town, Rosemary," Esther said. "We dated in high school."

"He's terribly good-looking," Rosemary said. "Sort of Latin looking like that old-time movie star, Rudolph Valentino."

Esther carefully wiped off a fingernail. "I think so, too. But Mother and Daddy don't like for me to date Tony because his folks were immigrants." She smiled, as though at a secret. "But what parents don't know won't hurt them, I always say."

Rosemary was a little surprised by Esther's attitude, knowing that she was an only child and the pride of her doting parents, but she said nothing. She finished the last nail and held her hands out for her roommate's inspection. "All right, Esther? I never seem to get polish on straight."

Esther said that it looked fine. She leaned back to let her own nails dry. "My folks have a dull boy all picked out for me at home. He wears glasses, and all he talks about is making money. He's a drip of the first order!"

Rosemary said comfortingly, "Maybe your folks will come around, Esther." Something in her roommate's demeanor distressed her. She seemed so flippant tonight.

Nancy stuck her head in the door. "Jumping Jehoshaphat! Aren't you two slowpokes ready yet?" Nancy was resplendent in a royal-blue dress that set off her red hair to advantage. "I've been ready for a half-hour." She was sporting a huge gardenia corsage. "See what my date sent me? Doesn't it smell scrumptious?" She whirled around the room ecstatically, and the heady fragrance sifted to the corners.

Esther and Rosemary admired the corsage extravagantly. Rosemary was sure that Gray would not bring her flowers, knowing his always-desperate lack of money. But I don't really care, not really, she told herself stoutly. I just hope he's been able to scare up something decent to wear, that's all. But it would be nice to have flowers, just once, from a boy she liked, she couldn't help thinking wistfully.

Rosemary's eyes were caught by a glittering bracelet on her friend's right arm. "Stop, silly goose," she said, grabbing at Nancy. "Let me see your bracelet."

Nancy stopped whirling and held out her arm. "I guess you're the only one who hasn't seen it, Rosemary," she said. "I wore it to the Homecoming Dance last semester."

Rosemary examined the bracelet. It was a gold-leaf design, set with seed pearls, sapphires, and chip diamonds. "It's exquisite," she breathed, "simply exquisite, Nancy. Wherever did you get it?"

Nancy beamed with pride. She held up her arm and let

the gems catch the light. "My grandmother gave it to me. It's the only nice piece of jewelry I own. Mr. Lawrence keeps it in the safe between wearings."

"It's the prettiest bracelet I ever saw," Esther said. "I could honestly steal it, Nancy."

"Say, don't be getting any ideas like that, girls," Nancy said good-naturedly. "Good thing Mr. Lawrence has a strong safe or I'd be minus one bracelet."

They all laughed, and at that moment the doorbell rang. Fern, who had been assigned to answer the door, called upstairs, "Rosemary Rossiter, your date's here."

Rosemary took one last look in the mirror, patted her hair, swirled her full green skirt to see how it would look when she danced, and went downstairs.

Was this really Gray waiting under the hall light? Rosemary had never seen him look so utterly smooth. Gray wore a dark-blue suit, a striped gray tie, and a white shirt; his unruly hair was slicked down for once; and he was holding a small corsage box.

His eyes lit up when he saw Rosemary, and he whistled meaningfully under his breath. "The little queen of Lawrence House," he said half-teasingly, but she knew he liked the way she looked. "Here, this isn't much." He held out the box. "But I hope you like it, Rosemary."

She took the box, murmuring, "Gray, you shouldn't have!" Inside the green florist's paper was a tiny corsage composed of two deep-red rosebuds, a delicate spray of white baby's breath, and four blue violets. It was tied with a fine white ribbon on a red paper heart encircled by a white frill.

"Oh, Gray, it's darling!" she said, glowing. "So dainty

and sweet." Something about the flowers made her want to burst into tears. She lifted the corsage out of the box carefully and held still while Gray pinned it on her shoulder. She tried not to wince when he stuck her a couple of times with the corsage pin.

Gray touched Rosemary's nose with his finger and smiled down at her. Her heart skipped a beat. "Sweet and dainty, like you," he said softly. "I'm glad you like it, Rosemary. I wish it could have been orchids, but you know the state of the stock market." He quirked his left eyebrow humorously, and she smiled back at him. For a suspenseful moment they looked deep into each other's eyes. Then the spell was broken when someone laughed in the lounge.

Rosemary tucked her hand into his elbow. Gray didn't look nearly so ordinary when he was dressed up, she decided. He had an air of gentility and a singularly gentle smile for a boy.

"Come on in, Gray," she said. "You'll probably know most of the girls." She hoped no one would be so ill mannered as to snub Gray because he worked in the Lawrence kitchen. The only girl who might would be Beverly.

Fern and Wilma were already in the lounge, Fern with the short, fat boy Rosemary had seen doing card tricks in Howley's. Wilma was hanging on the arm of a dashing man-about-the-campus type and already making eyes at him.

The two girls reacted graciously, as though they had never seen Gray washing dishes. Introductions were made all around and they sat down to await the others. Suddenly the doorbell began to clang, clang, and it seemed as if everyone's dates were arriving at once.

In a few minutes the lounge was filled with couples. Mr.

Lawrence came in, bowing all around with his old-fashioned courtly manner, and the girls introduced their dates to him. He shook hands with each boy, his goatee fairly bristling with cordiality. Then Alicia started the juke box, and the festivities began.

Rosemary noted with inner amusement that Beverly's date was fully as good-looking as Thad Thompson, who was dancing with Alicia, but that Beverly smiled alluringly at Thad every opportunity she had. Every time Rosemary thought to look, Beverly and her date were dancing close to Alicia and Thad. Beverly never gives up, Rosemary thought. Beverly had greeted Gray coolly, and Rosemary held her breath for a horrible moment, thinking Beverly was going to make a cutting remark about kitchen help, but she didn't.

Esther danced by with Tony and lifted her hand. They made a handsome couple, Rosemary thought, Esther so tiny and fragile, Tony so virile. But Esther had a surprising strength of mind underneath the fragility, Rosemary had already discovered in living at close quarters with her.

Surprisingly, Gray was an excellent dancer. In fact, he knew more of the current steps than Rosemary did. She had learned to dance in gym class at high school. On the few occasions when she had danced with boys at school parties, they had, to a man, walked on her feet and swung her about unrhythmically. She had long ago decided that dancing wasn't much fun, after all.

"Where did you learn to dance so well, Gray?" she asked after a particularly well-executed Charleston. She had been proud that the other couples had drawn back and left the middle of the floor to them. Beverly had looked at them with undisguised astonishment and had made a laughing remark to her partner. Something catty, I'll bet, knowing her, Rosemary thought.

"My mother used to be a dancing teacher, Rosemary," Gray replied. "You'd never think it to look at me, would you?" His eyes sparkled with suppressed humor. "Mom quit after she married Dad and they moved to the country. But she still practices on anybody she can lay her hands on. She's never gotten far with Dad, but she started on me young."

How full of surprises he is, Rosemary thought as they whirled down the room. Every time I see Gray, I find out something new about him. He's really an interesting and versatile boy. She gave herself up to the moment, to the pleasure of dancing with an unusually good partner.

"Are you having fun?" he whispered in her ear.

"Oh, Gray," she replied, "I don't know when I've had so much fun in my whole life!" He squeezed her hand.

The girls all look so pretty tonight, Rosemary thought, even Fern, who wore a little discreet pink make-up and a dress that was a little less frumpy than usual. She and the fat boy were jogging up and down the room in a straight line and looked as though they were thoroughly enjoying themselves, in spite of the fact that the other couples had to move out of their unwavering path.

The Chinese lanterns cast a rosy glow over the lounge and there was the blended scent of the corsages and the girls' perfume. It's so thrilling to be a freshman in college, Rosemary thought dreamily, to be dating a nice boy like Gray, to be living in the best house on the campus. For once she felt as though she really fit into the picture, too;

that she was like the other girls, the girls who had money and social position and both parents living and beautiful clothes and poised, assured manners; all the things Rosemary had envied in other girls and which she always felt had precluded her from being accepted as one of the crowd.

They stopped by the punch bowl for some of the delicious fruit punch that Lee Ann and Donna had concocted from a recipe of Donna's mother. There had been a great deal of giggling and sampling in the kitchen while they made it.

Gray ran his finger under his collar. There was perspiration on his forehead. "Wonder how Nellie's getting along," he whispered. "Maybe I ought to run out and give her a hand." He was teasing, but Rosemary took him seriously.

"Now, Gray, not tonight. We'll all have to wake up soon enough tomorrow and get back to work." She nibbled on a cookie while they watched the dancers. Thad Thompson was dancing with Beverly now, and she was turning on the full force of her most come-hither looks. Thad looks just like a charmed cobra, Rosemary decided. She wondered where Alicia was.

Rosemary and Gray had just decided to sit down when Rosemary felt a hand on her elbow. It was Alicia, looking rather serious. "Could you step outside a moment, Rosemary?" she asked quietly.

Rosemary excused herself and followed Alicia out into the hall. "What's the matter, Alicia?" she asked.

"Esther's sick upstairs. I knew you'd want to know."

Rosemary remembered how pale Esther had looked when they were getting dressed. "Of course. I'll go right up," she said.

The two girls hurried upstairs and went into Esther's and Rosemary's room. Esther was lying on the bed, still wearing her white dress. The exotic fragrance of her gardenias contrasted strangely with her white face.

Rosemary leaned over her. "Esther, dear, what's wrong? Can't we call a doctor?"

Esther shook her head and turned her face toward the pillow. "I'm just sick . . . at my stomach. It isn't anything to worry about."

Rosemary and Alicia looked at each other, and Alicia shook her head. "I certainly think we ought to call a doctor and call your folks, too, Esther," she said gently.

Esther's head shot up and she cried out, "No, don't call them, Alicia. I'll be all right. I've been like this before." She sank back against the pillow.

Rosemary nodded. "That's right, Alicia. She was sick in the night recently. She took a couple of aspirins and felt better in the morning."

Esther raised her head again. "Please tell Tony to go on home," she said weakly. "Tell him to call me tomorrow."

Alicia said, "All right, I'll tell Tony what you said, Esther, but I think you should let me call the doctor."

Esther shook her head stubbornly. "I don't want a doctor, Alicia. Please!"

"I'll tell Gray where you are," Alicia said to Rosemary, and left the room.

At Esther's insistence, Rosemary brought two aspirins against her better judgment. She wiped her roommate's forehead with a wet washcloth. Silently she watched Esther, but Esther had closed her eyes. She opened them suddenly and looked up at Rosemary. "Can you keep a secret?" she asked tautly.

"Why, of course I can, Esther," Rosemary replied, amazed at her roommate's strange manner.

"I've just got to tell somebody," Esther said, twisting her hands. "I simply can't keep it to myself any longer. I'm sure it's the nervous tension that keeps making me so sick. I'm so mixed up inside." She leaned closer, and her voice fell to a whisper. "You've got to swear you won't tell anybody."

"I promise I won't tell anyone," Rosemary replied. She smoothed back Esther's disheveled hair from her damp forehead. Esther looked at her and must have been satisfied that she could trust her, for she blurted out, "Tony and I ran away and got married in August, just before school began. My folks would be furious if they knew. They'd make us get an annulment, I know." Rosemary started to protest, but Esther rushed on headlong. "Today I got a letter from home. My parents want me to leave Waverly next semester and transfer to a girls' school in the East. I'm sure they suspect something. Oh, Rosemary, I just can't leave Tony! I just can't! I love him so!"

CHAPTER 7

A Bracelet Disappears

ROSEMARY'S ATTENTION WAS DIVIDED BETWEEN WHAT PRO-
fessor Hayworth was saying and dreamily watching the sun-
light touching Gray's head. It made the golden lights in his
brown hair glisten. He really is much better looking than I
first thought, she decided for the tenth time.

Gray glanced up suddenly and caught Rosemary watching him. He smiled, his eyes lighting up with the warmth
they always showed when he looked at her across the classroom. She smiled back, rather flustered, and hastily returned her attention to Professor Hayworth, who was lec-
turing on corrective speech this morning.

"Recent surveys show that more than two million public
school children have serious speech handicaps," he was saying portentously. "Of these, only about seven thousand
children are actually receiving speech correction. Those
who are not will undoubtedly go through life with speech
difficulties and resulting personality maladjustments. Children do not ever outgrow real speech disorders, contrary
to popular belief. A lisp or a stammer that was cute in a
child is far from cute in an adult."

Professor Hayworth turned a page. He was a small man
with thinning hair and a military mustache and bearing.

Rosemary knew that he was considered an outstanding figure in the field of speech, for he had written textbooks on all phases of speech work and was a pioneer in the field of speech correction.

Professor Hayworth continued in his precise diction, "It is the classroom teacher who must watch for the speech-handicapped student. While she is not capable of correcting speech defects which are of organic, psychological, or neurological origin, without the aid of a specialist, she can help those whose handicaps are of the 'bad habit' type." He looked up from his notes and Rosemary felt his keen eyes were boring through her. "The great need today is for more responsible, intelligent students to enter this field. The speech-correction teacher must not only have an understanding of speech and speech-science techniques, but he must understand the individual and have an insight into his problems."

By now Rosemary was listening raptly. Professor Hayworth had the knack of making the driest facts and statistics sound interesting. He lapsed into a more conversational tone and laid his prepared notes aside. "Probably some of you freshmen are not even aware that Waverly has a functioning speech clinic, of which we are justifiably proud. Each week a number of children enter the clinic for diagnosis and treatment. Our speech majors assist in this work. Remarkable success has been attained in many instances."

Professor Hayworth leaned back and put his hands behind his head. "One of the most interesting cases we are treating at present is that of a five-year-old boy whose problem is infantilism, or, in the vernacular, 'baby talk.' A senior major has been tutoring this child since the beginning of the second semester. We hope to have him talking plainly by the time he enters school in the fall."

Michael, of course, Rosemary thought, remembering the little boy Alicia was tutoring.

A serious-looking student held up her hand. "What kind of preparation does a speech correctionist have to have, Dr. Hayworth?" she asked. "It sounds very interesting."

The professor beamed and nodded. His eyes burned with the enthusiasm of the zealot. "You're right, Miss Adams. It is an interesting and gratifying profession. To answer your question. A speech correctionist must pass a speech and hearing examination himself; a course in speech fundamentals such as this one; possibly with electives in extemporaneous speaking; oral interpretation; advanced public speaking; debating; public discussion and dramatics. Then definitely phonetics; speech sciences; the principles of speech correction; and clinical practice. Then there are the teacher training courses which every teacher must take, educational psychology, plus the course for the teaching of speech itself. Of course this program differs somewhat according to the college, but it is broadly the same."

Another student questioned, "But, sir, don't the hospitals have facilities for speech correction?"

Dr. Hayworth shook his head. "In a few instances, yes, but the number of these clinics is unfortunately far too limited. The burden of speech correction, thus far, has rested on the schools themselves. The importance of correcting speech defects has become so important that clinics have been organized as a part of many educational systems."

Dr. Hayworth's eyes lightened and he chuckled. "I'll be perfectly honest with you, class. I hope every semester, by giving this lecture, to interest freshmen who haven't decided yet on a major to enter this field. If any of you are interested, feel free to visit the speech clinic after school or on Saturdays. I'm sure you'll become fascinated when you see the work being accomplished there."

The bell rang, and the class began gathering up their books. After Professor Hayworth dismissed them, Gray hurried over to Rosemary.

"Hi, Rosemary. How's Esther feeling?" he asked. Rosemary had not seen Gray since the dance the previous Friday night. When she had gone downstairs and told him Esther was ill, he had offered to leave so she could stay upstairs with her roommate. Rosemary had thought for a brief, dizzy moment that Gray was going to kiss her good night. But he had straightened up and plunged out into the night with his usual half-running gait.

"She's all right now, Gray," Rosemary said. "It must have been the excitement. Esther's rather nervous, you know." She felt herself blushing because she was telling him less than the truth, and also because she remembered how she had leaned forward expectantly thinking he was going to kiss her.

"That's good. I'm glad it wasn't anything serious. Esther's a nice kid." They walked out into the hall. "That speech-correction stuff sounds good, doesn't it?" he said. "I'd be tempted myself, if I hadn't already decided on veterinary medicine."

"Yes," Rosemary replied. "I'm becoming more and more interested in it. You know, Alicia is the senior he was telling about."

"It's something like my line, isn't it? Doctoring kids' speech—doctoring sick animals?"

She smiled up at him. "In a way it is. They're both worthwhile professions." They sauntered on down the hall.

"I have a report to write this afternoon," he said. "I'll see you at the house tonight, not socially, of course."

Rosemary realized that he was always bringing up indirectly his work in the kitchen. Did Gray feel self conscious about it on her account or was he really joking? She wasn't sure yet, but she wanted him to know that it made no difference to her that he had to wash dishes to help pay his expenses.

They parted at the door and Rosemary walked back to the house. She glimpsed Esther and Tony talking on the bench before Samuel Waverly's statue. Somebody had finally removed the school pennant from his hand and replaced it with a cigar. Rosemary's thoughts returned again to the rapid events of the weekend. It had been like a crazy quilt, like the Drunkard's Path pattern that her mother had quilted once, zigzagging here and there.

After Esther had confided her secret to her on Friday night, Rosemary had thought seriously for a long moment. Then she had said, "The only thing to do, Esther, is to tell your folks about your marriage. Don't you think they have a right to know?"

Esther had set her lips stubbornly. "They'd want to snatch me out of school right now, Rosemary. You don't know how they are. I've never been allowed to make any decisions for myself—not even what dresses I wanted to buy."

Rosemary had smoothed her roommate's hand. "Esther,

75

be sensible. Tony and you are married. You have been for more than six months now. Your folks can't do anything about it now, I'm sure. Does anyone else know?"

Esther had shaken her head. "Nobody but you. That's why I haven't been going home weekends. I've been spending them with Tony in his folks' cabin at Echo Lake. They don't know we're married, either. They're dreadfully old-fashioned and foreign in their ideas. I know they wouldn't approve." She had flopped over and buried her head in the pillow. "I wanted to stick it out and finish this year, but I don't know, Rosemary. I'm so upset all the time for fear someone will find out. And what if I should get pregnant? Tony's just got to finish school. I don't know what to do."

Rosemary had reiterated patiently, "There's only one honest thing to do, Esther, and you know what that is." She couldn't help feeling that Esther should have known better than to get married secretly when they both had college to finish. She had brought her problems on herself. Still, Rosemary felt sorry for her.

Rosemary had helped her roommate off with her clothes. Then she had undressed herself and gone to bed. She had thought about Esther and Tony. Their marriage had been foolish, but now that they had gone so far they couldn't turn back.

The dance music from downstairs drifted up to the two girls. The sounds of gaiety seemed incongruous in the somber quietness of the dark room. Esther was crying softly into her pillow. Rosemary listened to the muffled sound until she finally fell asleep. She dreamed fitfully all night, as she always did when she had a problem on her mind.

The next morning Esther made no reference to the previous night and Rosemary was glad not to have to discuss it any further. At breakfast Esther passed her sickness off as too much excitement.

Both she and Rosemary stayed at the house for the weekend while they worked on notebooks for botany. They went to the library on Saturday afternoon to look up some reference material. When they returned to the house for supper, Alicia met them at the door.

"Come into the lounge, girls," she said crisply. "Mr. Lawrence wants to talk to everyone."

"What's wrong, Alicia?" Esther asked lightly. "Somebody late getting in after the party last night?"

"I don't know, Esther," Alicia said evasively. "Mr. Lawrence just told me to call everyone together."

They walked into the lounge, where the other girls, conversing in low tones, were gathered. Rosemary and Esther sat down on the davenport and Rosemary glanced around the room. No one had gone home for the weekend because of the dance and the necessity for cleaning up afterward. There had been a tacit agreement that everyone would stay around the house to do her share.

Mr. Lawrence came in then and shut the folding doors into the hall. He had an unusually businesslike air about him. Everyone looked up expectantly, wondering what it was all about.

He took a stance before the fireplace and looked around the room as though he were taking count. Satisfied that everyone was present, he said, "I shall come directly to the point, young ladies. Sometime between last night after the dance and this afternoon there has been a third theft in this house."

77

A horrified murmur rose up all over the room. The girls looked at each other and then dropped their eyes. Rosemary sensed a growing tension in the room, a kind of universal embarrassment.

Mr. Lawrence continued, "Miss Potter wore an heirloom bracelet to the dance last night. You probably all noticed it. Afterward she dropped it in her dresser drawer intending to return it to me for safekeeping. It slipped her mind until this afternoon. When she went up to get the bracelet, it had disappeared."

Rosemary glanced over her shoulder at Nancy, who was sitting on the window seat. She had never seen Nancy look so serious.

"Good grief, Rosemary," Esther whispered. "Remember what I said last night about wanting to steal Nancy's bracelet?" Her face was red with embarrassment.

Rosemary nodded and whispered back, "Don't worry, Esther. Nancy knew you were just joking."

When the outbreak of comment died down, Mr. Lawrence went on, "Young ladies, this situation is becoming serious. We have in this house a thief or a kleptomaniac or someone is entering the house from outside. I only hope it is the latter rather than the former."

But Rosemary caught the doubt in his voice, and she knew everyone else must have, too. She looked around the room thoughtfully. There was a dead silence except for the sound of rain spattering against the windows. Everyone was looking tense and uneasy and carefully avoiding one another's eyes. Rosemary knew the same thought was flashing through all of their minds. That it must be one of themselves who was the thief! Who else would have known about the bracelet? Who else would have had the opportunity to enter Nancy's room? Certainly it would be impossible to get into the room through the upstairs window.

"Every girl in the house had an opportunity to take the bracelet, objectively speaking, of course," Mr. Lawrence said, fingering his gold-rimmed spectacles. It was obvious he found his task extremely distasteful, for it was well known that Irving Lawrence looked upon his "young ladies" paternally. "If the guilty party would only replace the bracelet, it would save everyone trouble and embarrassment. Otherwise, I must call in the sheriff again." His tone was regretful, his eyes sad.

Alicia spoke abruptly. "May I say something, sir?"

"Of course, Miss Barnes," Mr. Lawrence replied. He looked relieved at her interruption.

Alicia stood up and faced the girls. She took a deep breath. "I suggest that the sheriff not be called until tomorrow morning. If someone here did take the bracelet, let's give her a chance to make restitution. Sometime before tomorrow morning she could leave the bracelet where it would be sure to be found."

"That's a good idea, Alicia," Nancy said quickly from the rear. "I don't want to prosecute anyone. All I want is my bracelet back."

"But what about my pen and pencil set?" Beverly interposed in a cross voice from the chair by the fireplace. "I've never gotten that back, you remember, Alicia."

"And my fifty dollars too, Alicia," Lee Ann added meekly.

"That's true," Alicia said slowly. "But let's give the culprit one more chance. What do you say, girls?"

79

There was a chorus of agreement. Mr. Lawrence nodded benignly. "That's fair enough, Miss Barnes. I appeal, therefore, to the guilty person, if she is present, to leave the bracelet in the open where it can be found."

But by the next morning, Sunday, the bracelet had not turned up, and the sheriff was called again. During the afternoon each girl was summoned to the lounge and questioned privately. At supper, Mr. Lawrence reported that the sheriff had found nothing, not one clue, but he would continue to work on the case.

That night Nancy came into their room where Esther and Rosemary were lying on their beds in their pajamas, talking idly.

"Honestly, I do feel like a heel, causing all this disturbance," Nancy said, sinking down on the foot of Rosemary's bed. "But, flying grasshoppers, I hated to lose that bracelet. It's the only really nice thing I own."

"Nobody blames you, Nancy," Rosemary said. "After all, you had to report it."

Cynthia stuck her head in the door at that moment. "Guess what? My dad just called, gals. He and Rhea are coming over after me next Friday and we're all going to Columbus to the ice show. Rhea has a cousin at Ohio State she wants me to meet, too. She says he's simply super." Her eyes sparkled and she looked like a different girl from the listless and melancholy one Rosemary had first met.

"That's wonderful, Cynthia," Rosemary said. "I hope you have a grand time." She and Cynthia exchanged a glance of secret understanding.

The other girls echoed Rosemary's statement. "Well,"

Nancy said, when Cynthia had breezed out and they heard her go humming down the hall. "Did you ever see such a metamorphosis in anybody in your life? She's been about to talk my ear off lately. Sometimes I wish I had my old quiet roommate back. I like to do all the talking myself."

Rosemary smiled, knowing Nancy didn't mean it. She considered Cynthia's improvement her one accomplishment since she had been at Waverly. Now, if she could just do as much to improve her own personality, Rosemary thought.

Esther returned to the subject of the bracelet. "Who do you think took it, Nancy?" She added with an embarrassed laugh, "Of course you know I was only kidding when I said that about stealing it."

"I know that, Esther," Nancy said reassuringly. "Honestly, I haven't the faintest suspicion. I just hope it turns out to be some stranger, some second-story man."

Rosemary and Esther nodded, but Rosemary had her secret doubts. It just seemed highly improbable that anyone could have broken into the house without anyone's being aware of it.

"Did you hear the latest?" Nancy asked, changing the subject, her hazel eyes merry again. She swung her legs over the end of the bed. "Guess who's coming to favor us with a visit?"

"Who?" the other two girls chorused.

"The one and only Melissa Meadows! What do you want to bet she'll have along one poodle, one secretary, one maid, umpteen press agents, and her fourth husband?"

Rosemary felt a twinge of sympathy for Lee Ann, who

rarely mentioned her mother's name and always avoided any discussion of her movie career. "How do you know, Nancy?" she asked.

"Lee Ann got a wire from her mother awhile ago. She's back from her European honeymoon and they're driving through to the coast. They'll probably arrive tomorrow around noon, it said."

"Holy cow!" Esther said inelegantly, sitting up straight, her eyes wide. "You mean Melissa Meadows herself is coming right here to Lawrence House? I used to belong to one of her fan clubs."

"The very same of Hollywood and Broadway and other points," Nancy said. "But Lee Ann isn't much excited about it. I don't think she likes her mother very much, if you ask me."

The ten-o'clock bell clanged downstairs and Nancy shot for the door. "Sweet dreams," she said. "Lock up your socks full of money."

Rosemary threw a pillow at the door and Nancy dodged. "You look guilty, my friend," she said over her shoulder. "You have that kleptomaniac expression."

Still laughing, Rosemary turned back into the room. Esther was lying on her back staring at the ceiling with a rapt expression. "What I would have given two years ago to see Melissa Meadows in person—just my right arm, that's all! That all seems sort of silly, doesn't it, now that we're grown up?" But her voice was wistful and belied her words.

"Sort of," Rosemary agreed, but she was secretly excited about meeting the famous actress face to face. That night she dreamed of herself costumed in a white satin dress, long white gloves, and the traditional ostrich plumes, curt-sying to a glittering creature who vaguely resembled the Queen of England. Except that under each arm Melissa Meadows carried a white poodle, both dogs barking sharply and unceasingly.

CHAPTER 8

Enter a Movie Queen

BY MORNING THE NEWS WAS ALL OVER LAWRENCE HOUSE about the impending arrival of Lee Ann's glamorous mother. Everyone was talking about it but Lee Ann, whose habitual attitude was one of preoccupation anyway.

During the morning, while Rosemary had a free period, she went downstairs to the library basement to look for a book in the stacks. Coming around a dark corner, she almost stumbled over Lee Ann kneeling down looking for something on the bottom shelf.

"Oh, hi, Rosemary," she said, straightening up. "It's like the tombs down here, isn't it?"

"It certainly is, Lee Ann. Next time I'm going to bring a lantern."

Lee Ann smiled agreement, and Rosemary went by, finding the book she wanted. She went up the back stairs, so she did not have the occasion to pass Lee Ann again. At noon she noticed idly that Lee Ann was not at lunch, but it was not unusual for a girl to be missing at noon because of the classes and meetings which sometimes extended through the lunch hour.

They were just eating their dessert of bread pudding when Nellie came into the dining room moving faster than was her custom. She leaned over and whispered something in Mr. Lawrence's ear. He thanked her and turned to the girls. His calm voice, nevertheless, betrayed an inner excitement.

"Miss Meadows just called from a restaurant in town, young ladies. She'll be right out." He looked around the table worriedly. "Dear me, our Miss Meadows isn't here, is she? This is unfortunate."

Donna, Lee Ann's roommate, replied, "I don't think she has any class or meeting today, sir. But I have no idea where Lee Ann is."

Irving Lawrence frowned. "Miss Meadows mustn't miss her mother's visit. Does anyone have any idea where she might be?"

No one said anything. Suddenly Rosemary remembered seeing Lee Ann in the library that morning. It could be possible she might be working on a report that entailed a great deal of research. Rosemary decided she had better say something. "I saw Lee Ann this morning, Mr. Lawrence, in the library. Would you want me to run over and see if she's still there?"

"Certainly, Miss Rossiter. She'll be heartbroken if she misses her mother. Miss Meadows told Nellie over the telephone that she could stay only a short while."

The girls were all twittering, and Irving Lawrence was giving them some fatherly, if misguided, advice on how one should greet a celebrity as Rosemary ran upstairs to get her coat.

She was just coming downstairs when the doorbell chimed imperiously. All the girls dashed from the dining room and lined up in the hall expectantly. Irving Lawrence followed, trying to appear his usual dignified self, but Rosemary sensed that he was inwardly as thrilled as the girls.

Nellie, who never wanted to miss anything, pushed through the line of girls and threw open the door, a toothy, welcoming smile on her homely brown face.

Rosemary paused at the bottom of the stairs. She couldn't very well dash out right in their visitors' faces, she told herself. Truthfully, she knew she couldn't bear to leave without first seeing the entourage. And an entourage it was, something like the one Nancy had predicted. A haughty-looking woman in a severely tailored suit, holding a brief case and wearing harlequin glasses, faced Nellie. "I'm Miss Potts, Miss Meadows' personal secretary," she announced grandly. "We have the correct house, do we not?"

"You shore do, honey!" Nellie cackled. "Come on in and meet everybody!" Nellie stepped back and planted herself right by the door. The secretary faced about and stood at attention opposite the line of girls as though she were preceding royalty.

Next came a harried-looking little man wearing a beret and carrying a camera over his shoulder. He scanned the group speculatively.

"This is Cornelius Rhodes, Miss Meadows' press agent," the secretary announced. The man nodded shortly in the general direction of Irving Lawrence and the girls and began jotting down notes in a notebook he took from his pocket.

Then a faintly repressed, admiring gasp issued from the girls as Miss Meadows herself entered. She was just as beautiful as she appeared in the movies and on television, Rosemary decided. Platinum-blond hair flowed down gently to her shoulders. She was hatless and was wearing a pastel mink coat which was the exact shade of her hair. Her spectacular, heart-shaped face was artfully made up. She looked much too young to have a daughter who was a sophomore in college.

Rosemary almost laughed aloud when she saw that Miss Meadows was, indeed, carrying a toy poodle under her arm, but only one, not two as Rosemary had dreamed. It was a spoiled-looking little beast, wearing a jewel-studded collar, and was barking unceasingly.

Miss Meadows paused dramatically inside the door, smiled the lovely, slow smile that had brightened a million screens, and said in a throaty voice to the poodle, "Hush, Sesame! Hush! Look at all the pretty girls lined up to meet us."

She turned the full force of her neon smile on Irving Lawrence, who was already looking completely bedazzled. "And you must be Irving!" Miss Meadows said caressingly, as though she had made a wonderful discovery all by herself. No one dared to call Mr. Lawrence Irving, not even his closest friends. The girls all managed to conceal their amusement as Mr. Lawrence sprang forward and took the hand that Melissa extended graciously. At a glance from Melissa, the tailored secretary sprang forward and took Sesame, who had finally stopped barking.

"How do you do, Miss . . . uh . . . Mrs. . . . Miss Meadows," Mr. Lawrence said, bowing almost to his waist. "Welcome to Lawrence House. We are indeed honored, indeed."

Miss Meadows glanced behind her. "Now what has happened to Anthony?" she said. "An-thony, come in, dear."

She turned to Mr. Lawrence. "Anthony Lombard, you know," she cooed, "my husband." A flash of annoyance showed briefly on her flawless face as Melissa Meadows turned to look behind her. She cast an exasperated glance at her secretary. "An-thony, we're wait-ing!" she called.

All the girls were craning their necks to see the fortunate bridegroom. There was a moment of stunned silence when Anthony finally stepped through the door, looking like a steer being hauled to the slaughter. He was a stockily built man, partly bald, with a distinct tendency to fat around the middle.

Why, he's homely and old! Rosemary thought with dismay, at least fifty, not at all like a movie star's husband ought to look. Right now Mr. Anthony Lombard looked decidedly uncomfortable.

"An-thony, darling, do come in and meet Irving Lawrence and all of these lovely girls," Melissa sang out, her good humor restored.

Anthony shook hands with Mr. Lawrence and murmured something briefly while all the girls held their breath. Nancy winked at Rosemary, and Rosemary had to repress a giggle.

It was only then Melissa Meadows realized that Lee Ann was not among those present. "Why, where's my little girl?" she asked. "I thought that she'd be here waiting for us. Anthony's so anxious to meet Lee Ann." Anthony looked anything but anxious, Rosemary thought.

Golly, I almost forgot, Rosemary thought. She dashed through the group and heard Mr. Lawrence begin making hasty explanations to Lee Ann's mother. He gave Rosemary a dark look as she brushed past.

"Miss Rossiter," he hissed. "I thought you left long ago."

"I'm sorry, Mr. Lawrence," she said, swallowing. "I just wanted to—"

"Well, be on your way, and I'll speak to you later," he said. "You've held things up long enough."

The dog started to bark shrilly. The press agent had taken out his camera and was asking everyone to line up for pictures. The girls were talking now, and it was a complete hubbub. Rosemary was glad to get out into the fresh air.

She ran across the campus as fast as she could, almost colliding with the jolly fat boy who had dated Fern for the Valentine Dance. He reached out an arm to steady her. "What's the big rush, Rosemary?" he asked. "Going to a fire or just an exam?"

"Neither. I'm looking for someone," she shouted as she hurried by. He looked after her, grinning, and shook his head in mock despair. When she came to the library, Rosemary ran up the steps, glanced over the first floor, and then went down to the basement to the corner where she had seen Lee Ann. There was a dim bulb burning at the end of each long aisle, but no Lee Ann. Suddenly Rosemary remembered the quiet lounge on the second floor for those who wanted just to sit and think or to read without any interruption. Lee Ann might be there, Rosemary thought, and climbed the stairs to the second floor. By this time she was growing tired and there was a tight band around her chest from having run so hard in the cold.

She pushed open the door of the little room which was tastefully decorated in soft, pleasing shades of blue and gray. There were only six easy chairs and they were all unoccupied except one. Lee Ann was sitting with her eyes closed, a book lying open in her lap. She opened her eyes when Rosemary bent over her.

"Lee Ann, your mother's here," Rosemary said, anxious to deliver her message and get back before she missed something. "She's waiting for you. I thought I'd never find you."

Lee Ann looked at her strangely and didn't budge. "Is she?" she said coolly. "Well, I couldn't be less interested. I'm sorry you found me."

Rosemary stared at her friend, dumfounded. "Why, Lee Ann Meadows, what's the matter with you, saying that about your own mother? You should be ashamed of yourself."

Lee Ann didn't look at all ashamed. In fact, she looks downright spunky for once, Rosemary thought. I didn't think she'd ever show that much spirit.

"I'm sorry you went to so much trouble, Rosemary," Lee Ann said quite pleasantly. "I stayed away from the house purposely today. If I hadn't used up all my cuts in my three-o'clock class, I'd have gone into town." She looked down at her hands, the long, dark eyelashes so much like her mother's a faint shadow on her cheeks. Her voice had a ring of bitterness. "As far as my mother is concerned, I'm surprised she even bothered to stop. She hasn't been to see me for over a year now. And if she thinks I'm going to fall all over Anthony whatever his name is, she's badly mistaken."

Rosemary sank into a chair, too surprised to utter a word. She stared at Lee Ann, who stared back at her defiantly. This certainly wasn't the reaction Rosemary had expected. Lee Ann was well liked at Lawrence House in spite of her being a celebrity's daughter. She had never tried to take advantage of her position or the fact that she, along with Beverly, had far more money to spend and nicer clothes than the other girls. Rosemary was at a loss to know what to say.

"But they're all waiting, Lee Ann," she said helplessly. "They're just standing there waiting for you. Your mother said she couldn't stay long. Don't you think it would be dreadfully rude not to even go to see her?"

Lee Ann smiled maddeningly and leaned back in her chair. "Probably the only reason she even bothered to stop was so she'd get some free publicity," she said coldly. "There'll be pictures in the college paper of Melissa Meadows honoring a little fresh water college with her presence. Well, I don't want to be any part of it!"

What did you do in such a situation? Rosemary thought desperately. She tried to make her voice gentle. "Your stepfather . . . uh, Anthony Lombard, didn't look so bad, Lee Ann. I felt rather sorry for him, if you know what I mean."

For the first time Lee Ann showed regret. "Yes, I do know what you mean, Rosemary, and to tell the absolute truth I feel sorry for him, too." Then her voice hardened again. "Did you know that my father was the first Mr. Melissa Meadows? A talent scout saw Mother in a drugstore and offered her a screen test. As soon as she made her first big picture, she divorced Dad. That was when I was eight years old. Since then she's been married twice before this Anthony. I wanted to live with Dad all the time, but my mother always insisted I spend part of my time with her. I've been dragged all over the country on movie locations. Then Mother dumped me here. This past year she was so busy with her career and going to Europe and getting married again that she didn't want to be bothered with me. Now she's trying to make it up, pretending she really wants to see me. Just tell her you couldn't find me."

Rosemary realized, then, that Lee Ann's belated show of independence was a way of hurting her mother as she herself had been hurt for so long. She must really love her mother in spite of what she had said.

Rosemary didn't try to hide her exasperation. "I'm not going to lie for you, Lee Ann. I think your attitude is all wrong. After all, she is your mother, and she did take the trouble to come here. She wouldn't have had to drive through Waverly. It's off the main road." With that, Rosemary went out and let the door slam after her. The librarian gave her a reproving glance as she went by.

Now what was she going to say when she got back? Weren't people strange? They didn't react at all as you expected. There were hidden depths in everyone, she was discovering. You thought you knew someone and then you realized you didn't at all. Lee Ann, who had all the material advantages, lacked the one thing that would make her happy, the steadfast love of a mother who would be there when she needed her. At least I have that, Rosemary thought. Here I've been feeling so sorry for myself because I lost Dad, but I do have a wonderful mother that I can always depend on. Some girls don't have that much. But maybe Melissa Meadows does love Lee Ann in her own way, she thought, trying to be fair.

Rosemary had passed Samuel Waverly's statue and Lawrence House was in sight when she heard the sound of foot steps behind her. She turned. It was Lee Ann. Well, of all things! Rosemary thought. Now what's going on?

Lee Ann looked at Rosemary sheepishly and swung into step beside her. "I . . . changed my mind, Rosemary," she said unnecessarily. "You shocked me into it. I realized how abysmally rude to everybody it would be for me not to show up. I promise to . . . to act as though I'm honestly glad to see all of them."

Rosemary grabbed her arm, gave it a squeeze of approval, and they covered the remaining distance in a few seconds.

When they opened the door, Rosemary saw that the crowd had moved into the lounge. The photographer and a reporter from the school paper had arrived and were taking pictures of Melissa sitting on top of the piano. Mr. Rhodes was barking staccato directions at everyone. Anthony was chatting comfortably with Mr. Lawrence in a corner. The girls were sitting about watching the proceedings in an awed silence. Sesame was lapping up a bowl of milk while Miss Potts stood in close attendance.

When Melissa spied her daughter sidling in the door she jumped down gracefully and ran forward with her arms open. "Darling! I thought you'd never come! How is Mother's little girl?"

As Rosemary stepped back, trying to make herself unobtrusive, she glimpsed the expression of maternal affection on Melissa's face. She does love Lee Ann, she really does, Rosemary thought. It isn't only for publicity, after all. For the first time she felt a real liking and sympathy for the beautiful actress.

"Hello, Mother. I'm sorry I'm late," Lee Ann said shyly, and they embraced. Melissa turned toward Anthony, who stepped forward rather reluctantly. "And this is Anthony, dearest. I know you're going to like each other." Her tone was hopeful, almost pleading, as she looked from one to the other.

Rosemary felt her heart tightening. There was something pathetic in the scene, something that almost brought tears to her eyes. The room was silent, and everyone was watching intently. Anthony smiled and put out his hand.

"Hello, Lee Ann," he said in a low voice. "Your mother has told me so much about you. And of course she has your pictures everywhere."

Lee Ann swallowed and pasted a bright, welcoming smile on her lips. Probably only Rosemary knew what she was really thinking, how she was feeling inside. Lee Ann's putting up a good front, Rosemary thought in admiration, just as she promised.

"Hello, Anthony. I'm so glad you came, so we could finally meet," Lee Ann said cordially. "Won't you both come up to my room where we can talk privately?"

"Of course, darling," Melissa said quickly, showing obvious relief that the meeting had gone off so well. "Miss Potts can take Sesame out for a little run and Cornelius can do whatever he wants. Of course we can't stay long, you know," she added hastily. "I'm making a personal appearance tonight in Columbus, so we'll have to be running along."

"Certainly, Mother, I understand," Lee Ann said, and the three of them went upstairs.

With the departure of the star of the event, the silence dissipated and the girls all began to chatter at once, comparing their reactions. Irving Lawrence disappeared into his office. Miss Potts snapped a jeweled leash on Sesame's collar and they went outside, the little dog nipping at her heels. Cornelius Rhodes engaged the school photographer and reporter in agitated conversation.

Rosemary went up to her room, smiling to herself. Things had really turned out much better than she had expected. The smile faded when she remembered that Mr. Lawrence was going to speak to her later. She had just opened her history book when Alicia came in and said Mr. Lawrence wanted to see Rosemary.

So Rosemary trailed downstairs, her heart pounding, and knocked on the door of his office. He opened the door at once and said, "Sit down, Miss Rossiter." She could tell that he was still displeased with her. She sat down by his desk and he gave her a brisk lecture on the ability to follow directions promptly and cheerfully.

She sat with a noncommittal expression on her face, but she couldn't help thinking how funny Mr. Lawrence's goatee bobbed when he talked so sternly.

When she left, she had five more demerits, which, added to her ten previous ones, confined her to quarters for the weekend. "I take special interest in you, Miss Rossiter," he said in parting, "because you are Caroline and Leon's niece. I had hopes of developing you into one of our finest products." Although she was smarting from his lecture, she thought he made it sound like a piece of cheese the house was turning out.

CHAPTER 9

A Surprise for Rosemary

WHILE MELISSA MEADOWS HAD BEEN UPSTAIRS IN LEE ANN'S room news had sifted to the far corners of the campus that she was at Lawrence House. When she left, bestowing smiles and kisses and breathless thank yous upon everyone in sight, a crowd had gathered before the house waiting to get a glimpse of her.

It was plain to Rosemary that Melissa was extremely gratified by her warmhearted reception on the Waverly campus. Her "Good-by, darling. Write to Mother," floated back as the cream-colored Cadillac with Sesame barking nastily out of the window drove off slowly down the street.

Lee Ann stood looking after the car with an unreadable half-smile on her lips. She turned toward the house and sighed. Once again the wistful expression settled over her pretty countenance.

Feeling sorry again for the girl, Rosemary whispered, "How did you like Anthony, Lee Ann?"

She replied wryly, "Oh, he wasn't so bad, I guess, better than the last one anyway. At least he treated me like an adult and not like a little girl. He didn't bring me a baby doll like the last one."

Rosemary restrained an impulse to put her arm around

the other girl, for Lee Ann was the sort who wouldn't want pity expressed openly. It was unlikely she would ever again refer to what she had told Rosemary in a burst of confidence at the library.

Two days later, when the college paper came out, there was a wide spread of pictures of Melissa, with her poodle, with her new husband, with the Lawrence girls, on the piano alone. It was ironic but fitting, Rosemary noted, that Lee Ann did not appear in any of the pictures.

The latest robbery at Lawrence House had all but been forgotten in the light of the more exciting events. Indeed, it was as though nothing had been stolen. One day Rosemary passed the sheriff leaving the house, but no mention was made by Irving Lawrence of the fact that he had been there again.

Everyone was concerned now about the coming midterm exams. Fern was tutoring Wilma nightly, and Wilma confided to Nancy that she would almost as soon flunk out as have to keep to the grindstone that way. Life wasn't worth living when you didn't have any fun, she groaned.

Esther was still sniffling into her pillow almost every night but unbearably gay around the other girls, Rosemary noticed. Rosemary often saw her and Tony in conversation about the campus. Esther had not yet told her parents of her secret marriage, she informed Rosemary. Rosemary withheld comment. She had offered her honest opinion to Esther; there was no more she could do. Esther would have to work out her own personal problem, that was certain.

The days seemed to be flying by in a kaleidoscopic dream as far as Rosemary herself was concerned. She met Gray for cokes at Howley's and for brief whispered colloquies at the library. She wrote long letters to her mother and read her mother's letters with lessening pangs of homesickness. Her mother wrote that Mr. Fisher and she were seeing a great deal of each other. She was anxious for Rosemary to meet him, perhaps on her next visit home.

Rosemary realized, with a sense of astonishment, that she was becoming orientated to being away from home, that she was gaining in social poise and the social graces, in knowing how to get along with other girls, and how to accept those who had all the advantages she had always envied so much. It had been a good experience for her to come to Lawrence House, she admitted to herself. To find that all her material possessions did not make a Beverly Coleman likable; that an attractive girl like Lee Ann could suffer pangs of insecurity and fear. That Esther, only child of doting parents, was straining desperately at the bit of parental domination. Yes, she was maturing in more ways than one, Rosemary decided, even though she did seem to get into trouble.

Now, if she could only make plans for the next semester. But, she reasoned, how could she even decide on a major when she wasn't sure she'd return to Waverly? Uncle Leon had been so positive that she would be able to work out her future if she only had a push in the right direction. But the old ever-present problem of money was still staring her in the face. She was sure her grades would not be good enough to apply for a scholarship. The mid-term grades would be an indication where she stood.

Whenever she was free, Rosemary began accompanying Alicia to the speech clinic, watching Alicia's patient work with Michael, watching her make tests of the pathetic, afflicted children brought in by anxious parents, watching her record the piping voices, test hearing capacity, and perform all of the other functions that were a part of the speech clinic. Professor Hayworth noticed Rosemary's frequent appearances at the clinic and spoke to her one afternoon. "Think you might like to join up with us in the speech department, Miss Rossiter?"

She looked up shyly at the man whom she admired and respected so much. "I'm not sure, sir. I haven't selected a major yet and I'm very much interested in speech work. But. . . ." Her voice trailed away. She hated to admit her financial problem to anyone, especially Professor Hayworth.

"But what, Miss Rossiter?" he persisted. She had the feeling his all-seeing eyes saw right through her.

"I'm not sure I'll be returning to Waverly, sir," she said, deciding to be frank. "It all depends on whether I can find a job and earn my tuition."

"I see," he said thoughtfully. "You're a good student, Miss Rossiter. You have a natural aptitude for speech work. I can see that from your performance in public-speaking class. I'd like very much to see you go on. We can use students like you. Have you thought of applying for a scholarship?"

"Yes, sir, I have, but I don't think my grades will be good enough. I've always been terribly average, Professor Hayworth. I know there are many others much smarter and more deserving than I am."

He smiled. "Don't ever sell yourself short, Miss Rossiter. Remember that you have as much chance as the next student. In the meantime, feel free to come around the department all you want, see what we are doing. I can recommend some good books for you if you wish to do some reading to help you make up your mind. And there are other fields of speech which might interest you, too. They all dovetail together. It's a wonderful subject, you know." He inspired her even further with his own enthusiasm, and she resolved to follow his advice.

Soon thereafter Rosemary went around to the college theater and sat in the back row watching rehearsals. The drama classes were getting ready for their spring production of *You Can't Take It with You.*

She haunted the library lecture room where the debate teams were preparing for the biggest tournament of the season at Manchester, Indiana, debating on the subject of "Public versus Private Water Power." Thad Thompson was one of the varsity debaters, Rosemary found. As she listened to the debates, she wondered how Alicia and Beverly were working out their romantic rivalry over Thad.

She listened attentively while Professor Hayworth and his assistant coached the entrants for the intercollegiate interpretative reading contests. She attended the panel discussions of campus problems sponsored by the public discussion class. She carried home armloads of books from the library and decided to write her term paper in freshman English on America's greatest public speakers. But always in the back of her mind was the problem of whether or not she was doing all of this work and research in vain. And was it fair to her mother for Rosemary to want to finish college when it was such a struggle for Frances Rossiter even to make ends meet? Was Rosemary being selfish and self-centered?

Rosemary and Gray were discussing their respective plans for the future one day in Howley's. "I finally have a job lined up for the summer, Rosemary," he was saying enthusiastically. "With a vet not far from home, a Dr. Fosdick. It'll be good experience for me. Of course I won't actually do any work on the animals, but I'll keep the kennels clean, feed the animals, and can observe his treatment methods."

"That's wonderful, Gray," Rosemary said, happy for him. She sighed. "I just wish I was as sure about my summer. You are planning to come back to Waverly, aren't you, Gray?" She realized his answer was supremely important to her.

"Sure I am, Rosemary, for the second year of my pre-vet course," he replied. "Then I'll apply to Ohio State or Cornell for acceptance to their veterinary college. That's a four-year course, you know. Probably after that I'll intern for a year with a vet, maybe this Dr. Fosdick, if he'll have me. Provided, of course, I pass the state board requirements."

Rosemary felt a sinking in the region of her heart at the thought of Gray's going away to another college for four years. Four long years! Why, in that time he'd probably meet some other more attractive girl and forget all about her. The thought made her utterly miserable.

However, she pretended an enthusiasm she didn't feel so that Gray would never suspect her feelings. "Just think, then you'll be Dr. Horton, Gray!" she said. "You'll probably have so many patients you'll have to get an assistant right away."

Gray laughed even though he looked pleased at her faith in him, and put his hand over hers. "Don't jump so far ahead, Rosemary. It takes a vet a long time to get established. Don't forget he can't send his patients off to a hospital the way another doctor can. He has to buy all his hospital equipment himself, the X-ray machines, the kennels, the buildings to house the animals. Plus the fact that he has to find an area that needs a vet." He looked at her teasingly, his gray eyes twinkling, and rubbed his ear lobe with his thumb. "Think you'd want to be married to a vet, Rosemary? You'd be competing all the time with his patients for attention."

His tone was bantering, but she could sense the seriousness behind it. Her heart almost missed a beat. Was Gray proposing? Or was he just being curious? She chose her answer carefully. "Any girl should be proud to marry a vet, Gray. It's a very honorable profession."

He laughed, and the breathless moment was gone. "Ha, so it's the profession that's appealing, not me? Well, I guess I can take a hint." He put her coat around her shoulders and held back her chair. "Time to head off toward the Lawrence kitchen, Rosemary. Nellie's probably got a stack of dishes a mile high waiting. She's a hard taskmaster, but we get along fine."

That night Frances Rossiter called long distance. Rosemary's heart throbbed when she heard her mother's voice. She hadn't realized how homesick she was to hear it again.

"How are you, honey?" her mother asked, her voice coming thin over the wire, as though she were across the continent and not less than a hundred miles away.

"Fine, Mother! Just fine!" Rosemary replied. A long-distance call always excited her. "I'm studying for midterms. How are you getting along?"

"Right as rain, dear. Keeping busy, of course. I've that blouse almost finished I promised you." Her mother paused, and her tone changed. "Rosemary, would you be able to come home this weekend? Mr. Fisher said he'd be glad to drive over for you Saturday morning if you could come. I'd ride along, of course. Then he'd drive you back Sunday afternoon."

Rosemary's heart sank. She would love to go home, but she had already promised to take tickets at the basketball game Saturday night.

"Golly, Mother, I can't." And she explained her predicament. Her mother thought a moment. "Perhaps we could drive over Saturday and see you then. I haven't seen your room yet, and I'd like to meet Esther and the other girls."

Rosemary thrilled at the prospect of her mother's actually coming to Lawrence House. "Why, of course, Mother. You and Mr. Fisher plan to eat supper with us, too."

"I won't promise about the supper, Rosemary, but we'll come soon after lunch. If anything should happen we have to give up the trip, I'll call you."

After Rosemary had hung up, she returned to her room with a smile playing around her lips. She had the feeling that her mother had some special reason for wanting to see her this weekend. Could it have anything to do with the mysterious Mr. Fisher?

Saturday loomed a bright azure blue and unusually warm for March. There was a definite hint of spring in the air, and everyone at Lawrence House looked happy and energetic at the reprieve from the cold and dreary days. Even the prospect of the mid-term exams coming up next week failed to put a damper on the girls' bubbling spirits.

Rosemary was disappointed to find that Frances Rossiter would not be meeting Esther, after all, for she and Tony were leaving after breakfast for his parents' cabin at Echo Lake. Only Rosemary knew this fact. To Alicia and Mr. Lawrence Esther said merely that she was going home for the weekend. Lee Ann was visiting Donna's family in the southern part of the state. Beverly was expecting her father to pick her up in his private plane for a weekend trip to New York. Fern and Wilma planned to spend the weekend at Fern's home boning up for exams. Cynthia had a weekend party date with her stepmother's cousin at Ohio State. So only Rosemary, Nancy, and Alicia were left in the house.

"I'm simply dying to meet your mother," Nancy said as she and Rosemary cleaned Rosemary's room. Rosemary had already helped Nancy clean hers, since both their roommates had begged off their part of the cleaning task.

Rosemary flashed a grateful look at the other girl. You could always depend on Nancy to be agreeable and enthusiastic about everything, she thought. "I'm glad there's going to be someone around for Mother to meet, Nancy," she said. "I know she's going to be disappointed so many of the girls are away."

She pushed the vacuum cleaner over the green rug while Nancy dusted. Both wore blue jeans, a costume not permitted on the campus and worn only in the privacy of Lawrence House when no visitors were present. They would have to change before they could go down to lunch. The two girls made a pleasing contrast, Nancy with her red hair and blue shirt; Rosemary with her brown hair and daffodil-yellow blouse.

"Are you worried about mid-terms, Nancy?" Rosemary asked. For all her lightheartedness and jollity, Nancy was a serious student, and was majoring in pre-med.

"Only about that darned Latin," Nancy moaned. "I just can't get languages—never could. And if I flunk, I'll have to repeat it, too."

"I know what you mean," Rosemary sympathized. "Grammar never did make heads or tails for me, not even English grammar. I think I'll do all right except for botany. I just have to have that science credit."

"Oh, you'll get along all right," Nancy said comfortingly, as she wiped off the dusty windowpanes. She leaned back to admire her handiwork. "You just don't have enough self-confidence, that's all. You always think you're worse than you are in everything."

Nonplused by Nancy's candid remark, Rosemary stared at her friend. "Whatever do you mean by that, Nancy?" she asked, putting down the vacuum cleaner.

Nancy fixed her with a keen but friendly eye. "Come now, Rosemary. You know well enough what I mean. You always underrate yourself in everything. You think everybody's smarter than you, prettier than you, better off than you. In fact, you like to wallow in self-pity."

Rosemary flushed. Nancy had put her finger pretty well on her inner lack of security. Rosemary couldn't really take offense at what her friend had said. It was all too true, she had to admit.

"I suppose you're right, Nancy," she said lamely. "I've always been like that. And I think more so since my father died. That knocked the props right out from under me. We were awfully close, you see. I'm always afraid . . . well, that people won't like me, Nancy?"

Nancy finished her dusting with a flourish and threw herself down on the bed, propping her legs up on the footboard. "Don't you realize everybody feels that way some time or other?" she said emphatically. "I do. Even a girl like Beverly does. That snootiness and arrogance of hers are just a cover up for something, you can bet your last dollar on that. You're no different from anyone else, Rosemary. You probably just attach more importance to your feelings and worry over them, that's all."

Rosemary said rather haughtily, "I didn't realize you were such an amateur psychologist, Nancy. You ought to charge for your character readings." She was more than a little humiliated that Nancy had seen through her outer veneer so accurately. Nancy just smiled. Rosemary thought of the girls in the house who had confided in her and she knew that Nancy was pretty nearly right in her analyses.

"And the biggest fear of all is in the mind of the girl who's been stealing from the rest of us," Nancy continued, more seriously now. "That must be an awful thing to have on your conscience." She laced her hands behind her head and grinned. "I've always fancied myself an amateur detective, too, among my other accomplishments. But I admit I'm stumped on this case."

At that moment the warning bell for lunch rang and the moment of introspection was over. Both girls scrambled to get rid of their blue jeans. Rosemary put on her navy skirt and the red sweater which her mother had always liked on her. Then she and Nancy went downstairs. The dining room looked empty with only the two of them, Alicia, and Mr. Lawrence for lunch.

"My young ladies are certainly depleted today," the old gentleman said. "This is the least number we've had for a meal this semester."

They had barely finished lunch and Nellie had cleared the table, when the doorbell clanged. Rosemary ran to answer, sure that it must be her mother. And she was right, for there was Frances Rossiter in the familiar blue velvet coat and toque which made her look like a bluebird, a red scarf at her neck. Rosemary was vaguely aware of a tall man behind her when she said, "It's so good to see you, Mother!"

When they drew apart from their embrace, Frances turned to the man behind her. "This is Jesse Fisher, Rosemary." The tall, thin man with the intelligent brown eyes, the graying temples, and the sensitive mouth smiled down at Rosemary rather uncertainly, as though not sure of his reception.

Why, he's nice and even rather handsome, Rosemary thought. His eyes seemed to approve of her as she shook hands with him. "She's just as pretty and wholesome looking as you said, Frances," he said.

Rosemary twinkled demurely at him and turned to her mother. "Don't you both want to come in?" she said. "Mr. Fisher can sit in the lounge while I take you upstairs and show you my room, Mother. No men are allowed upstairs except relatives."

They stepped inside, and Rosemary introduced them to Irving Lawrence, who appeared promptly. Then Rosemary took her mother upstairs, leaving Mr. Fisher and Mr. Lawrence conversing. When she introduced Nancy and Alicia, Rosemary was pleased to note that both girls looked impressed by her mother's attractive appearance.

After her mother had seen her room and the four of them had talked for a few moments, Rosemary and her mother rejoined Jesse Fisher and Mr. Lawrence. The latter tactfully excused himself and withdrew to his office.

Frances and Rosemary sat down on the davenport while Mr. Fisher faced them from an easy chair. He asked permission to light his pipe and leaned back, smoking contentedly. He looks to be about forty, Rosemary thought. He had an easy, uncomplicated manner which went with his faintly shabby tweed suit.

"How do you like Waverly, Rosemary?" he asked, showing a sincere interest while she replied that she liked it a lot. "It's my alma mater, too," he said. "Quite a while ago, though. In fact, my wife was a Lawrence girl. This house is an old stamping ground for me, although Mr. Lawrence didn't remember me at first. I guess I've changed some since then."

Her mother smiled. My, she looks well, Rosemary thought. She's even put on a little weight since I left. She doesn't look nearly so tired as she did for a while after Dad died. She didn't look at all embarrassed at Jesse's mentioning his wife.

"Did you come to Farmingdale High just this semester, Mr. Fisher?" Rosemary asked.

"Yes, I did, Rosemary. I took old Mr. Hanks's place when he retired. It was only a temporary appointment to finish out the year." They chatted idly for a few minutes about people at the high school whom Rosemary knew. Then she inquired, "Would you care to take a walk around the campus? And you will both stay for supper, won't you?"

"I'm sorry, dear," her mother replied. "Jesse has a class party to chaperone tonight and he invited me to go along. So we won't be staying long. But we did want to see you today."

A warning bell rang in the back of Rosemary's mind. Then they did have a special reason for coming, as she had anticipated. Jesse Fisher and her mother glanced at each other and her mother took a deep breath. She looks positively girlish and radiant, Rosemary thought. I never noticed before how pretty she really was when I saw her every day.

Jesse Fisher cleared his throat and studied the bowl of his pipe with deliberate intentness, as though he had never seen it before.

"Rosemary, I . . . we have something to tell you," her mother began falteringly, looking rather apprehensive. "Jesse . . . that is, Mr. Fisher has just had an offer from a high school in Fremont, Iowa, to come there as vice principal. It pays much better than Farmingdale and it's what he's always wanted, to be a school administrator. The job begins in June because the school office is open all summer. The thing is—" and her voice caught nervously. Then she continued, "Well, Jesse has asked me to marry him, Rosemary. We want to know how you feel about leaving Waverly and attending a community college in Fremont."

Rosemary was so shocked that she couldn't think of anything at all for a moment. She sat stunned, staring blankly at the two of them, her mouth frozen. Her mother getting married and going off to Iowa? She having to leave Waverly and all she had come to love there? What about Gray? What about her speech work? Some colleges didn't even offer a major in speech. All of these thoughts flashed through her mind in the moment of silence. She noticed with a part of her mind that the library clock was just striking three. The resonant tones seemed to echo and re-echo in the quiet room.

Rosemary moistened her lips. "I don't know what to say, Mother. I . . . well, I like it here. I've been thinking about taking speech." She realized she wasn't being very coherent. "About your getting married . . . I can't be selfish about that. I know you're lonely, but . . . ." She bit her lip. What could she say without hurting her mother and embarrassing Jesse Fisher?

Jesse took her up quickly. "But it's all such a new idea, isn't it, Rosemary? You don't know how you really feel about it." His tone was quiet and kind. "We knew it would come as a surprise, but we wanted to talk it over with you before we made a decision." He glanced at Frances fondly and she nodded back at him unobtrusively. "Perhaps you'd better have time to give this some thought, Rosemary. Remember, we want you with us if you want to come. You'll always be welcome in our home. But if you want to stay on at Waverly, that's up to you. We can help you partially, if you can finance the remainder of your expenses."

Rosemary looked at her mother searchingly. "You've

definitely decided, Mother, that you're going with Mr. Fisher?"

Her mother nodded, took off her white gloves, and held out her hand silently. On the wedding-ring finger was a square-cut diamond in an old-fashioned setting. "This was Jesse's mother's ring, Rosemary," she said proudly.

Rosemary's eyes went to her mother's right hand, where she was wearing the small diamond Phil Rossiter had given her. A sharp, biting spear of jealousy cut through Rosemary. Her father was already relegated to the past. How could her mother forget so soon when they had been so much in love? He hadn't even been dead two years yet!

"I know how you must feel, dear, all this coming so suddenly," her mother continued, looking at her with sympathy, "but Jesse has to give an answer to the superintendent of schools in Fremont. You do understand, don't you?" She glanced at her fiancé and Rosemary could see the affection between them. "I know you want me to be happy, Rosemary. It's been lonely for me since you've been away," her mother said apologetically.

Rosemary tried to smile even though there was a vast, empty space in the pit of her stomach and her eyes didn't seem to focus. "Of course, I do understand, Mother," she said, controlling her voice admirably. "You go ahead with your plans and don't worry about me. After all, I really won't have to decide until after this semester, will I?"

They left shortly thereafter, and Rosemary waved after them as they drove off in Jesse's middle-aged sedan. Then she ran upstairs, threw herself across her bed, and burst into the tears she had been holding back. She wasn't even sure why she was crying, whether it was for herself or for her father. Suddenly the day which had begun so happily had become intolerably dismal. She felt as though a precious era in her life had ended abruptly and that nothing would ever be quite the same again.

CHAPTER 10

Thad Asks a Favor

MID-TERM EXAMS WERE OVER AND EVERYONE AT LAWRENCE House breathed an enormous sigh of relief. Rosemary had achieved B's in all subjects but public speaking and botany. In the former, she received an A and in the latter, to her dismay, a C. But it took only a B average to make the Dean's List, so she had made it by the skin of her teeth. She knew her mother would be pleased. However, to apply for a scholarship, a student could have nothing less than a B grade in any subject, so Rosemary resolved to redouble her efforts in botany to bring her grade up to a B.

Even Wilma had managed to squeak through in everything, barely enough to be taken off probation. Fern self-righteously informed everyone that if it hadn't been for her coaching Wilma would have certainly flunked out. Even Wilma, momentarily subdued, agreed and said wearily she supposed all the cramming had paid off, after all, and that she owed Fernie a lot. But Rosemary had never seen Wilma look so tired and colorless.

Of the Lawrence girls, only Donna Farrell had earned A's in all subjects. "Jumping Jehoshaphat! Why wouldn't she?" Nancy declared vigorously to Rosemary. "Donna never does anything but study. She hasn't had but one date since she's been here, and that was the Valentine Dance and Alicia got her that one." Nancy herself had done well in all subjects but Latin, having gotten a C in that subject.

The two girls were whispering in the library in spite of pointed frowns from the librarian. "Let's face it, Nancy," Rosemary replied. "Donna's just brilliant, even though she isn't very attractive. She probably would make A's if she didn't study. Lee Ann said she was first in her class in high school, too."

Nancy sighed. "I suppose you're right, Rosemary. She'll probably be somebody we'll be saying 'we knew when' about someday." They both laughed at her wandering excursion through the sentence but Rosemary grasped her meaning.

All at once Nancy nudged her. "Look, there's Thad Thompson. Isn't he simply divine? I could run off to a desert island with him any day." Her tone changed to one of astonishment. "Why, he's heading over here!"

It was true that Thad was approaching their table with a friendly grin on his handsome face. "Hi, Nancy, Rosemary," he said. "Coming over tomorrow to the debate, Rosemary?"

Rosemary didn't dare glance at Nancy, but she knew the other girl was staring at her in amazement. "I didn't even know there was a debate scheduled for tomorrow, Thad," she replied. "What time?"

"Three o'clock. We're debating the last time before the Manchester Tournament. It's Hanover this time. They have a stiff team, too. Plenty of competition. Hope you get around to coming, Rosemary. You haven't missed many of our debates lately."

Rosemary smiled up at him, perfectly at ease before the round eyes of her friend. "I'll make it if I can, Thad. And thanks for inviting me."

He said, "So long," and sauntered off. Nancy whispered furiously to Rosemary, "Rosemary Rossiter, you little devil! You didn't tell me you knew Thad that well. Why, he's practically the most outstanding boy on the campus!"

Rosemary couldn't resist preening her feathers a little for Nancy's benefit. She spoke nonchalantly. "I've been dropping around and listening to the debate team, Nancy. Thad's debate manager and on the affirmative team. They usually don't have much audience, so I guess he couldn't help noticing me there."

"Well, if I'd known Thad was on the team, I'd been sticking along and sitting right in the front row," Nancy pronounced definitely. They both giggled and then subsided at another warning glance from the librarian.

Nancy began composing her weekly theme for English. Rosemary sat looking at her history book, pretending to be studying, but she was really thinking of the letter she had received from her mother that morning.

Jesse Fisher had accepted the position in Fremont, Iowa, and her mother had handed in her resignation from her office job for the middle of May. They were planning a quiet wedding in the chapel of the church Frances Rossiter had attended all of her life. Uncle Leon and Aunt Caroline would stand up with them. Probably it would be Memorial Day weekend, Frances had written, and they would take a brief honeymoon before driving on to Iowa. Frances was sorry that she would have to leave the state before the end of Rosemary's college year, she said, but Jesse was due to assume his new duties on June 8.

Well, that's that, Rosemary had thought upon finishing the letter. Her feelings were mixed with gladness for her mother's new-found happiness and uncertainty about her own future. She had told Gray this morning about the possibility of her transferring to the community college in Fremont.

She had been flattered by the look of acute disappointment that flashed across his face. "Why, you can't do that, Rosemary," he said. "You've got to stay here another year, at least, until I go to veterinary school. Why, Waverly wouldn't be the same place without you." He put his hand over hers, and her fingers thrilled to his touch. Gray wasn't usually very demonstrative, but she knew now that he genuinely liked her.

"I don't want to leave either, Gray," she said sadly. "I never realized how much I liked it here at Waverly until I thought I might be leaving. I suppose Mother would be happier, though, if I went to school in Iowa."

"Don't worry about your mother, Rosemary," he said rather bluntly. "She'll be so busy getting settled, getting acquainted, making a new life, she isn't going to need you."

Rosemary had to admit to herself that it was probably true. Her mother didn't need her so much now that she had Jesse Fisher. Their relationship probably never again would be as close as it had been in the interim since her father had died. Rosemary felt twinges of her old fear of insecurity. Now she would feel like a fifth wheel with her mother and Jesse. There would actually be no comfortable place for her in their new life together.

Rosemary suddenly realized that she hadn't read a word of her history lesson. She had better get busy, she told herself. She was already behind on her required reading for the course.

That evening after dessert Irving Lawrence arose at the table with a momentous air. He cleared his throat and polished his spectacles before he adjusted them carefully.

"Young ladies, you will all be interested in the contents of a communication I received today." Nancy grinned slyly at Rosemary from behind her water glass. She always said Mr. Lawrence could be depended upon to find a five-syllable word where a two-syllable one would do as well.

"The college authorities are instituting a new Good Citizenship contest which has rather unusual rules, yes, quite unusual. I shall endeavor to make them clear to you herewith." He took a sheet of paper from his pocket and glanced over the information while the girls waited with keen anticipation. Then he looked up and beamed impartially about the table at the candlelit faces.

"This contest is to select the boy and girl on the campus who are considered to have made an outstanding contribution to campus life in their respective domiciles. Each house may make one nomination which will remain secret until the final winners are announced. The sum and substance is that the girl must be the one whom you consider to have been the best citizen, to have made the most impact on life in Lawrence House during this year. It may be in the academic field"—here all eyes turned toward Donna—"or in social activities"—the girls glanced almost reluctantly toward Beverly who looked self-conscious—"in leadership"—

Alicia was the center of attention—"or for being helpful and friendly toward others. You each may write one name on the ballot with the reasons that you are nominating this girl. I also have a vote. I shall tally the votes and send to the dean the girl getting the most votes with the reasons for her nomination. From the names submitted from all of the houses and dormitories on the campus a faculty committee will select the most deserving boy and girl."

He paused tolerantly while the girls murmured excitedly to each other. Then he announced, "The prize for this Good Citizenship contest, young ladies, is one year's free tuition."

A babble of voices echoed this announcement. Rosemary felt a rising elation when she heard the liberal reward, but then her heart sank hopelessly. Looking around the table, she had to admit that she was, without question, the most ordinary and least deserving girl there.

Mr. Lawrence raised his hand to indicate quiet. "The voting will take place on April 15. The contest winner will be announced on Awards Day in May. In the meantime you can be observing and thinking about your choice."

Of course the topic of conversation around the house that night and in all of the houses on the campus was the contest. No one would admit whom she intended to vote for. Esther commented wryly to Rosemary after they had gone to bed that Beverly would undoubtedly nominate herself. They both laughed, but Rosemary decided that Alicia Barnes was going to be her choice.

The following afternoon after the debate, in which Waverly scored a decisive victory over the Hanover team,

Rosemary was putting on her coat when Thad came up to her. He had been easily the most outstanding debater of the four, and Rosemary couldn't help feeling a certain pride. After all, Thad was the boy friend of one of her friends, and that made her feel a kind of kinship with him.

"Just a minute, Rosemary, and I'll drive you home," he said in her ear. "There's no use your walking when I have the car."

Rosemary nodded, speechless at his unexpected suggestion, but she was thrilled at the prospect of riding in Thad's expensive foreign sports car, which was unique on the campus. She waited a little breathlessly while Thad shook hands with his opponents and rounded up his belongings.

He took her elbow as they walked out of the Law Building where the debate had been held into the lavender and rose-shaded dusk. The days were growing longer now that March was almost over, and a few hyacinths were peeping up through the shrubs that bordered the campus buildings. Rosemary took a deep breath, thinking how good it was to get out into the fresh air after the smoke-filled room. The little red car stood at the curb. Thad handed her in and took his place behind the wheel. She noted the fine leather upholstery and the expensive cut of Thad's topcoat. Everything about him spelled "money," the same kind of money that Beverly Coleman had.

Rosemary ran her hand over the seat, relishing the feel of the soft leather. She sighed unconsciously, wistfully. It would be fun just once, she was thinking, to date a boy who had plenty of money to spend, an expensive car, good-looking clothes. And then she scolded herself that she should be thoroughly ashamed. Such selfish thoughts were dreadfully disloyal to Gray.

The little car purred over the road toward Lawrence House at the other end of the campus. Rosemary sat up straight, wishing some of the other freshman girls could see her now, but not a one was in sight. That was always her luck, she thought. It was almost the supper hour, and the campus was practically deserted, the calm that descended on it every day before the evening classes began and the club meetings and the exodus to the reference room.

"Hanover was stiff competition. We were lucky to get the decision," Thad said. "Now on to Manchester! We've lost only two debates this year. We're hoping to take the tournament. Waverly hasn't won it for ten years."

"I hope so, too, Thad," Rosemary said. "Your team is excellent, I think," she added loyally. "I'd like to be on the debate team sometime if I ever become good enough."

He grinned. "Professor Hayworth always says debating takes brains first, speaking ability second, and looks third. You've got all three, Rosemary, so why don't you try out next year? He's always looking for good material."

"Maybe I shall, Thad," she said shyly. She was blushing, in spite of herself, at the compliment. Thad's so nice, she thought, not at all snooty as one would expect a big man on the campus to be.

He drove up in front of Lawrence House and parked. "I had a special reason for wanting to talk to you privately, Rosemary," he said, turning toward her. "It's about Alicia. I know you're good friends."

"Yes, we are," Rosemary said. She surreptitiously glanced

at her wrist watch. Supper would be in five minutes. She'd have to hurry or she'd earn a demerit for being late.

"It's kind of a favor I'd appreciate your doing for me," he said rather diffidently. "I don't have any sisters and my mother's in Kansas City, so she can't help me out. You see"—and he dropped his voice confidentially—"I'm planning to have a pearl set in a ring for Alicia for graduation, one my brother brought from Japan when he came back from the war."

"Oh, how nice, Thad!" Rosemary exclaimed, thinking how pleased Alicia would be.

"I don't know the ring size, though," he said, "and I need some feminine advice on the mounting. I didn't feel I could very well ask Beverly for any help." He smiled crookedly.

Rosemary's lips twitched. "Of course not, Thad, not Beverly," she echoed, knowing they understood each other.

"I was wondering if you could manage to get hold of a ring of Alicia's and measure it for me," he said. "I want it to be a surprise, and that's the only way I could figure out to do it. Then maybe you'd go with me to pick out a mounting." He gave a self-deprecating laugh. "I'm afraid I'm not much up on feminine likes and dislikes and I want it to be just right."

Rosemary felt immensely flattered that Thad would even confide in her and ask her advice. "Why, I'd be delighted to, Thad," she said.

He breathed a sigh of relief. "That surely takes a load off my mind, Rosemary. And please don't mention it to anyone, because I want it to be a real surprise."

"You can depend on me, Thad," she said. She heard the warning bell ringing for supper. She opened the car door.

"I'm sorry. I have to run," she said. "Thanks for the lift, and I'll let you know about the ring size as soon as I get it."

He turned on his motor and waved toward her. "I'll be seeing you soon, then, Rosemary," his voice rang out in the quietness.

As she turned toward the house, Rosemary almost ran headlong into Gray dashing around the corner. She realized at once, with a sickening sensation, that he had heard what Thad had said, for he had an unbelieving stunned expression as he looked after the car. As he brushed on by he said coolly, "Hi, Rosemary. Sorry I'm in a hurry. I'm late tonight."

Before she could even answer anything but, "Hi, Gray," he had run around the side walk and she heard the kitchen door slam.

Well! she thought with righteous indignation. He didn't even give me a chance to explain. Why shouldn't I ride home with another boy? Even if he did only want to talk about another girl's gift? But I'll just keep that part to myself, she decided. Just let Gray be jealous. He needs to thinks he has some competition.

With that comforting thought, she went in to supper. She could hardly keep from betraying her secret when she saw Alicia. What a nice surprise she was going to have, come graduation. Rosemary hoped that the pearl ring would terminate any further romance between Beverly and Thad. Rosemary wished she could tell Esther and Nancy about the ring, since they had been as interested as she in the triangle, but she couldn't break her word to Thad.

She noticed that Beverly, who rarely acknowledged her lowly freshman existence, kept looking at her speculatively and was blissfully unaware that Beverly had been standing in the window when Thad had driven her home.

After supper Esther had a freshman-class committee meeting to attend, so Rosemary was left alone. She sat down near the open door so she could see whether Alicia left her room. In a few moments she heard Alicia telling Donna that she would walk over to the library with her. Now if Beverly would just leave, Rosemary thought, I could get that ring size for Thad.

Alicia and Donna went downstairs. Rosemary kept watching, and presently Beverly came out of her room with her coat on and carrying a notebook. Good, she's going out, too, Rosemary thought. Things are working out just fine. The room opposite Alicia and Beverly's which was occupied by Nancy and Cynthia was dark. I'd better go now while I have the chance, Rosemary decided. She borrowed a tape measure from Esther's sewing kit and put it in her skirt pocket.

It was quiet now on the second floor, although Rosemary could hear muted voices from the lounge. She slipped down the hall and into the end room. As usual, Alicia's side of the room was in meticulous order and Beverly's was strewn with clothes, discarded copies of high fashion magazines, and jewelry tossed carelessly about. How typical of the two girls their room was.

Rosemary lit the light on Alicia's dresser and opened the upper drawer quietly. It was likely that any jewelry Alicia had would be there. Yes, there was a leather box. Rosemary opened it, and in orderly arrangement found earrings in one side, rings on the other side, and necklaces underneath on the lower level. She picked up a ring which bore a

Marine insigne. Alicia had shown her the ring once and said her brother had sent it to her when he was in the service.

Rosemary was looking at the Marine insigne when she heard an icy voice behind her. "What is the meaning of this?"

Rosemary whirled around in confusion. Wouldn't you know it? Beverly stood at the door, staring at her grimly.

"Oh, B-Beverly," she stammered, with a foolish half-laugh that she knew sounded idiotic. "I—I thought you were . . . were out."

"Evidently!" Beverly snapped. "Snooping, Rosemary, or just stealing?"

Rosemary flushed and dropped the ring like a hot potato back into Alicia's jewel box. "This isn't what it looks like, Beverly, I assure you," she tried to explain. And then she realized, with horror, that she couldn't even tell Beverly what she was doing. She'd be just mean enough to spill the secret to Alicia, especially when she discovered that Thad was the donor. So Rosemary finished lamely, "I was just . . . just admiring Alicia's Marine ring."

Beverly came over to the dresser and looked down into the box suspiciously, while Rosemary swallowed and edged toward the door. Beverly looked up, her lovely eyes cold. "You wouldn't be the little lady who stole Nancy's bracelet, would you?" she asked caustically.

Rosemary stared back at her, suddenly angry. "Beverly Coleman, what makes you ask a thing like that? You know I wasn't even living here when the robberies began!"

Beverly's lips curved upward in a taunting smile. "No, but that doesn't mean you couldn't have used those other robberies as an excuse to take anything you wanted. I've a good notion to call Mr. Lawrence." She moved toward Rosemary threateningly.

Rosemary felt like running, but she stood her ground. She tried to steady her voice. "Beverly, please don't do that," she begged. "I wasn't stealing. Really, I wasn't. And please don't tell Alicia you found me looking at her ring."

Beverly stood looking at her for a tense moment. Then she smiled, but there was no warmth in her smile. "All right. I won't tell anyone. This will be a little secret between you and me, Rosemary. Just remember that."

Rosemary muttered, "Thanks, Beverly," and fled down the hall. She shut the door into her room and stood against it, trembling. She had the feeling that she had not heard the last of this little incident. Beverly was just nasty enough to hold it over her head.

She flopped down on her bed, realizing with dismay that she hadn't gotten the measurement of the ring after all. Oh, dear, now she'd have to find another time to get into the room. If Beverly caught her again, Rosemary could imagine the consequences.

CHAPTER 11

A Mystery Solved

DURING THE FOLLOWING DAY, ROSEMARY WAS ABLE TO GET the measurement of Alicia's Marine ring while Beverly and Alicia were both in class. She told Thad when she ran into him in Howley's. He was pleased. "Some of the guys tell me there's a little place over in Richmond that makes mountings reasonably, Rosemary. How about riding over with me Saturday morning to pick one out?"

Richmond was the nearest big town, about fifteen miles to the east. "All right, Thad," Rosemary said, "but maybe I'd better meet you somewhere else, so Alicia won't see us together." Beverly, too, she thought worriedly, but she had thought it best not to mention their encounter to Thad.

So they arranged to meet at the library at ten o'clock Saturday. Their plan hung pleasurably in the back of Rosemary's mind during the rest of the week. It would be fun riding to Richmond with Thad in the cute little car. He was the smoothest boy she had ever known and a senior besides, and freshman girls were rarely seen with seniors.

Gray had been avoiding Rosemary since he had seen her that evening with Thad. He hurried out of public-speaking class and stayed out of her way at the house. She was amused and more than a little perturbed. After all, Gray had never even asked her to go steady, so he had no right to be offended or jealous. She certainly wasn't going to run after him to explain.

Of course, Saturday morning, as Thad was pulling away from the curb and Rosemary in her best spring suit was sitting beside him, who would have to come out of the library but Gray! He looked straight at them, and Rosemary couldn't help feeling sorry for him. He looked wistfully at Thad's car and his shoulders sagged. Rosemary lifted her hand and waved, but Gray pretended not to recognize her and stomped on by, his head bent and his eyes lowered.

"Isn't that Gray Horton, the dishwasher at your house?" Thad asked.

Rosemary nodded. "He was my date for the Valentine Dance, if you remember," she said clearly. "We've been more or less going together." She wanted to make that plain to Thad.

"Oh, sure, I do remember seeing him there. He was the good dancer, wasn't he?"

"Yes, he was. I do hope Gray didn't misinterpret our being together, Thad." In spite of her resolutions, her voice was concerned.

He grinned. "Don't you know yet a little competition is good for a guy once in a while? Let him think we're dating, Rosemary. It won't hurt him. Maybe it'll make him appreciate you all the more."

She smiled back at Thad, feeling better already, and they lapsed into a comfortable silence as they whizzed along. It was nice to be with a chap like Thad who had no romantic interest in her and for whom she felt only liking and admiration. Even though Thad possessed all the advantages that Gray didn't—and that she fervently wished Gray had—Gray was still first in her affections. Given the money, social position, and advantages that Thad had, Gray could be a big man on the campus, too, Rosemary told herself with fierce loyalty.

It was a gorgeous April morning as they left Waverly and began the drive across the flat, straight road toward Richmond. The fields were already showing a lettuce green, and here and there they passed a farmer plowing the fertile black soil. White farmhouses dotted the landscape. Rosemary felt suddenly homesick for Farmingdale. This country was the fabric of her life. Could she ever leave it to go hundreds of miles away?

She realized that Thad was talking again about his favorite subject, the varsity debate team, and she brought her wandering attention back to him.

"Are you going on to school after you graduate, Thad?" she asked.

"I've already been accepted at Harvard Law School, Rosemary. The only problem is whether Alicia will wait for me, or whether she'll want to get married right away."

"Have you asked her yet?" Rosemary dared to ask, since Thad had brought up the subject himself.

He shook his head. "My folks aren't too crazy about the idea of my getting married until I finish my law training. And you know that Alicia's planning to be a speech correctionist. She already has a job lined up in New York State. I don't know how we're going to work it out. But I'm going to ask her to marry me when I give her the pearl ring."

Rosemary was thrilled that she was the first to know. Another momentous secret she must keep to herself.

"How about you, Rosemary?" he asked. "What are your plans?" She was so pleased with Thad's interest that she found herself talking volubly, telling him all about her parents, about Jesse Fisher, about Uncle Leon and Aunt Caroline, about her interest in speech work, about her continuing at Waverly next year—everything that she had been bottling up within herself for so long.

All the time Thad kept nodding and listening and asking intelligent questions. Suddenly Rosemary realized she had been talking continuously most of the way. "My goodness, Thad!" she said, rather embarrassed. "You know more about me now than even my roommate does."

He smiled back at her. "It's good to talk to someone disinterested, Rosemary. You've heard that confession is good for the soul. Don't you feel better now?"

She had to admit that she did. There was something exceedingly comfortable about Thad.

They had reached the outskirts of Richmond, and Thad drove directly to the tiny shop which faced on the central square. A sign proclaimed in faded gold letters, "Jewelry Made, Bought and Sold."

An old man, presumably the owner, who looked as if he had grown up in the musty shop and had never been outside of its walls, waited on them. They looked at a variety of settings, and Rosemary finally selected one that she thought would suit Alicia, a plain yellow-gold setting, sleek and modern looking.

She walked away tactfully so that Thad could discuss finances with the old man and looked along at the jewelry displayed in the cases. The old man had quite a selection.

There was one case in which he displayed distinctive pieces he had made himself, another with nationally advertised brands, and another case which was labeled "Secondhand Pieces."

In spite of the unprepossessing appearance of the shop, Rosemary thought, he has nothing tawdry or cheap looking. Most of the secondhand pieces looked like family heirlooms. Probably someone had needed money badly, she mused, and had to dispose of the treasured old pieces.

She started to turn away when her eyes were caught by a beautiful bracelet that lay on a piece of dusty blue velvet in the bottom of the case. Her heart skipped a beat. She leaned over and looked at the bracelet closely. It was a gold-leaf design set with seed pearls, sapphires, and chip diamonds. Could it be . . . could it possibly be Nancy's bracelet? Rosemary stared at it with mounting excitement. If it weren't Nancy's, it was certainly an exact duplicate.

She saw that Thad had completed his business and was looking to see if she were ready to leave. She said casually to the old man, "That bracelet in the secondhand case is identical with one a friend of mine owns. Do you remember where this one came from? I know she'd be curious, because she thought hers was an original design."

The old man took the bracelet from the case and handed it to Rosemary for closer inspection. She was positive now that it was Nancy's.

"Let's see," he said slowly, scratching his grizzled head. "I bought that bracelet from a young lady. Said it was her grandmother's. I remember she hated to part with it, but she needed some money."

With difficulty Rosemary maintained an expression of only polite interest, although her pulses were throbbing. "Would you happen to remember what she looked like?"

The old man gathered his brows together in concentration. "All I remember she was one of them teen-agers. Had a scarf tied around her head. I ain't too observin' of young females. I got her name, of course. We have to register that for the state law."

Rosemary could hardly conceal her eagerness. She managed a casual half-laugh. "Would you mind telling me who it was? I'm interested so I can tell my friend."

She realized that Thad was staring at her, completely puzzled, but she simply had to follow through on this for Nancy's sake. She winked at him, mystifying him still further, while the old man dug out a musty black book and painstakingly ran down the lists written in an old-fashioned Spencerian script. His finger finally stopped. "Yes, ma'am, here it is. A Miss Betty Smith of Waverly College. I always keep accurate records."

Rosemary's heart sank. What a corny assumed name. She tried to keep the disappointment from showing in her voice. "And you're sure you don't remember what she looked like, sir?"

The old man shook his head. "No, can't say as how I do, miss. I ain't too good on faces any more. Just remember she was wearing a crazy outfit like them college girls wear nowadays—blue jeans, I think. I declare, they look more like boys than girls." He looked at Thad for confirmation, and Thad agreed solemnly, although his eyes were twinkling.

Rosemary thanked the old man and drew Thad out of

the shop. "What in thunderation was that all about?" he asked the moment they were out on the sidewalk.

Rosemary knew that the robbery stories had been kept as quiet as possible on the campus by the girls and the school authorities to save the fine reputation of Lawrence House. But she felt now that she had to explain to Thad. She told him the whole story after they had gotten in the car.

"I think you ought to go right to the sheriff, Rosemary," he said firmly. "This is a police matter. You can't do any more yourself."

But she was not wholly convinced. Her mind was working. Every girl in the house wore blue jeans and slacks at one time or another. Even Fern donned blue jeans for housecleaning tasks, although she always made apologies for them. And even if the old man were confronted with the correct girl, would he remember her? Were his memory and eyesight reliable enough to make a positive identification?

Rosemary shook her head. "I don't think I will just yet, Thad," she said stubbornly. "Maybe I can find out something more definite." A half-formulated plan was working in her mind which just might do the trick. "The important thing is to save the reputation of the house, Thad."

He obviously disagreed with her, but he subsided into silence. "Okay, it's your baby, Rosemary," he said. "You do what you think is right."

All the way home Rosemary was laying her plans to catch the culprit.

The first thing she did after lunch was to place a long-distance call to Aunt Caroline on their farm outside of

Farmingdale. After the amenities, Rosemary explained what it was that she wanted. Aunt Caroline at first thought she must be joking. But, being the good sport that she was, she finally agreed to cooperate.

"I promise nothing will happen to it, Aunt Caroline," Rosemary said. "And you'll really be doing a great service for Mr. Lawrence." Since Caroline had herself been a Lawrence girl, she could hardly refuse.

When she hung up, Rosemary sat back and smiled to herself. She sailed upstairs on fluffy clouds. When Esther said, "'What in the world is eating you? You look just like a Cheshire cat!" Rosemary simply smiled and said "Secrets!" and the frustrated Esther could get nothing more out of her.

After supper Rosemary sauntered down to the dining room and peeked through the swinging door. The house was almost deserted on this Saturday night, and it seemed lonely. Nellie was washing the dishes tonight alone, warbling "Sweet Kentucky Babe."

"Gray isn't here, Nellie?" Rosemary asked needlessly.

"No, he ain't, honey chile. He went home for the week end. He told Mr. Lawrence yesterday he was going. Didn't he say nothin' to you about it?" Nellie asked slyly. She had taken a great interest in their dating all along, and she must have been aware of the rift between them.

Rosemary hated to admit, even to Nellie, that Gray hadn't informed her of his weekend plans. In fact, she hadn't even talked to Gray since the night Thad had driven her home. But she said carelessly, "Oh, I forgot it was this weekend he was going," knowing she hadn't fooled the wise Negress at all.

"Better be nice to that Gray, Missie," Nellie warned sagely, her white teeth gleaming. "He's a mighty good boy— the kind that makes good husband material." She cackled.

Rosemary muttered, "Good night, Nellie," and fled. Why had she been so stiff-necked that she hadn't explained to Gray about Thad? Maybe right now he was dating another girl at home, someone he thought appreciated him.

Disconsolately, Rosemary decided to go to bed early and read a novel. Ordinarily, she had little time for light reading, but she had finished her preparation for Monday classes. The book was interesting, but Gray's face kept intruding between her and the pages, so finally she turned off the light and went to sleep.

The promised box from Aunt Caroline arrived on Tuesday well insured, carefully packed, wrapped, and sealed. Bless Aunt Caroline, Rosemary thought; you can always depend on her. She put the box in the back of her dresser drawer where no one could see it, until she was ready to use it. Wednesday night, she decided, would be the ideal time for her plan. There was an all-campus sing in the auditorium which most of the girls would be attending, so the house would be practically deserted.

Wednesday noon Rosemary made an elaborate ceremony of bringing the box to the lunch table and unwrapping it so that everyone could see. "It's from my aunt and uncle, you know. They're rather well off and don't have any children, and they've always been partial to me . . . ." She rattled on and on. She had made sure that every girl would be on hand for lunch today before she produced her supposed gift.

With fabricated delight, Rosemary lifted out the emerald-set wrist watch that Uncle Leon had given Aunt Caroline on their tenth wedding anniversary and which she wore only on special occasions.

A chorus of "oohs" and "ahs" echoed around the table. Even Beverly looked impressed for once. "Let us look at it, Rosemary!" Donna said, and her plain face showed unusual longing as she examined the beautiful timepiece.

The girls passed the wrist watch around the table and even Mr. Lawrence looked at it and pronounced, "A handsome piece, indeed. You must handle this carefully, Miss Rossiter. Is this your birthday?"

She had to tell a white lie because Irving Lawrence could easily see on his records that it was not. Under the circumstances, she felt the white lie was justified. "Aunt Caroline promised it to me when I graduated from high school," she trilled, "but she had to have some work done on it first. I'll keep it in my room to look at today and then I'll give it to you tomorrow, sir, to put in the safe."

When the girls got ready that evening to attend the sing, Rosemary put on her coat and walked along as far as the library. She and Esther had dropped behind the girls when Rosemary exclaimed as though she had just remembered, "Jeepers, Esther, I just remembered something I was supposed to look up for English tomorrow!"

"That's too bad, Rosemary," Esther said. "Maybe you can get around to the sing later. To tell the truth, though, I'm not staying long myself. Tony wanted me to meet him, so I'm planning to sneak out as soon as it gets started."

Rosemary dashed into the library via the front door, but, instead of staying, she went out the back door and hurried back to Lawrence House. When she opened the front door, she noticed that Mr. Lawrence's light was on in his office. Nellie was warbling "Steal Away to Jesus" in the kitchen. The lounge was deserted. Someone had forgotten to turn off the juke box and it was grinding out a noisy rock-and-roll selection.

Rosemary slipped upstairs, opened the door into her room without making a sound, and crept into the closet. She had left the watch still in the box conspicuously displayed on the top of her dresser. Several of the girls had been in and out of the room since lunch and had noticed it. Esther had warned her that it was foolish to leave it exposed like that, but Rosemary had said she liked to look at it.

The closet was hot and stuffy. Rosemary felt rather foolish huddled on the floor in the dark and hoped she wasn't going through all these theatrics in vain. It had been just seven fifty by the hall clock when she had come upstairs. If anyone was going to appear it would have to be soon, because the sing was supposed to end at nine thirty and the girls had to be back in the house by ten, as usual.

Rosemary had left the closet door slightly ajar. The full moon was shining in the window and slanted across the red bedspreads. She heard the library tower clock chime nine. She shifted her position and stretched out her legs, which were becoming cramped. The time was dragging tediously. She began wondering if she had been foolish to start this elaborate plan. She was going to feel idiotic if no one showed up tonight. She had already decided that, if her scheme fizzled out, she would go to the sheriff tomorrow with what she knew.

While she waited, Rosemary fell to thinking of Gray and their misunderstanding; of her mother and Jesse Fisher; of Cynthia and her new romance with her stepmother's cousin; of Lee Ann and her mother; until she had almost fallen asleep. Wouldn't it be a joke if she fell asleep and missed the thief and Esther came in and found her in the closet?

Suddenly Rosemary's senses quickened and she almost stopped breathing. She had heard a quiet movement in the hall, as though someone had hesitated and was looking around and listening. Then a call came softly, "Rosemary ... Esther," but she couldn't recognize the voice because it was so faint. She glued her eye to the crack and waited, her heart pounding.

After a tense moment the door opened quietly. A dark figure moved stealthily into the room. It was a girl, all right, but Rosemary couldn't tell which girl. The figure halted a brief instant, as though listening. Then she moved to the dresser and turned on a small flashlight.

If the moonlight were only shining on that section of the room, Rosemary thought. She could see the intruder's hands but nothing else. The hands snatched up the watch and fondled it. Then the figure switched off the light and started toward the door, her footsteps so faint they hardly made any noise at all.

All in one rapid movement Rosemary pushed back the closet door and reached out to the light on her desk. She had planned every action carefully. Light bathed the room. The girl stopped stock-still, her mouth frozen, her eyes extended, the emerald watch still dangling from her right hand.

It was, unbelievably, Fern!

CHAPTER 12

Rosemary Reveals a Secret

"I JUST DON'T UNDERSTAND IT, ROSEMARY," ESTHER SAID sleepily from her bed. "The pious Fern, of all people!"

"I felt the same way," Rosemary replied, turning on her side. "But I still can't help feeling sorry for her, Esther."

Esther yawned. "You really astound me sometimes, Rosemary. Imagine being clever enough to catch her right in the act!" The house was quiet now, and Fern had been taken off to the infirmary.

The plan had worked out just as Rosemary had hoped it would, and yet, when Fern had burst into helpless, wrenching tears, Rosemary had been sorry. She took the watch from the limp fingers and led Fern to the door. "Come, Fern," she said gently. "We'd better go downstairs to Mr. Lawrence's office."

Fern had still not uttered a word. She just stared dully at the floor. Somehow her long hair had become partially loosened from the bun and her plain face was splotchy red. Indeed, she presented a sorry appearance. She kept swallowing and sniffling and blowing her nose. By the time Rosemary had brought Fern to Mr. Lawrence's door, she wished passionately she had never become involved. The girl was so utterly pathetic.

"My dear young ladies," Irving Lawrence said in a shocked voice. "What is all this about, pray tell?"

Fern's body sagged while Rosemary explained briefly what had transpired. Mr. Lawrence looked at Fern as though he could hardly believe it. "Is this true, Miss Waterman?"

Fern's voice came from behind her sodden handkerchief. "Yes. I'm sorry, Mr. Lawrence. I wouldn't have done it if I hadn't needed the money."

"But, Miss Waterman, why didn't you explain your circumstances? I'm sure the college would have extended you a loan."

Fern looked up, and her eyes showed a spark of life for the first time. "I don't see that it makes any difference to the girls I took the things from, Mr. Lawrence. They certainly could afford to lose them, Beverly and Lee Ann and Nancy and Rosemary!" Her voice betrayed a sullen resentment which Rosemary had not heard before in it. She almost laughed aloud, wondering how Fern could possibly have gotten the idea that she was affluent.

Irving Lawrence, obviously still flabbergasted, was polishing his spectacles absently. "That isn't the point, Miss Waterman. You had no right to steal from your friends. You do see that, don't you?"

But Fern did not seem to see it. She tossed her head, and her voice was shrill. "You're a man, Mr. Lawrence. You can't understand what it's like—living with girls who have all the pretty things I never could have. My folks believe jewelry and pretty clothes and make-up and dancing are products of the devil. I just couldn't stand . . . being so different!" She started to sob. "Nobody . . . will . . . understand!"

Mr. Lawrence said quietly to Rosemary, "You'd better run along, Miss Rossiter. I'll have to call the sheriff and the school physician." He shook his head despairingly. "I'm sure Miss Waterman needs medical attention."

Rosemary nodded, cast one last, pitying glance at the distraught girl, and went upstairs. When Esther came in, she was already in bed, tired to the core. A nervous reaction had set in and she couldn't stop shivering.

"What's going on downstairs?" Esther asked. Rosemary felt there was no reason not to tell Esther what had happened, so she did so modestly, for Mr. Lawrence would tell Alicia and soon everyone in the house would have to know.

Wilma came into their room forlornly before bedtime. "Poor Fern. I wonder what will happen to her now." She sat down glumly on Rosemary's bed.

"Probably nothing too serious," Rosemary said comfortingly. "I doubt if anyone will press charges, Wilma."

"Except maybe Beverly. She'd be just stinking enough to." Wilma looked as though she might break into tears any moment.

"I guess we should have known right along," Esther interposed. "Fern never has seemed . . . well, quite normal."

"Fern's got a lot of good points even if she does look sort of drippy, Esther," Wilma fired back at her.

"Why, of course, she has, Wilma," Esther replied hastily, glancing desperately at Rosemary. "We all know that. There must just be a quirk in her mind, that's all. Fern isn't a bad girl."

Wilma looked mollified and left soon to go to bed. "Our room isn't the same without Fern," she said mournfully as she went out. "I miss her so much."

"Well, I'll be hornswoggled!" Esther said. "Wilma was eternally griping about Fern before!"

"I know it, Esther, but they needed each other," Rosemary said. Suddenly she felt much older and wiser than the demure Esther, even if Esther did have a husband.

Somehow, in spite of Mr. Lawrence's pleas to keep it quiet, the news spread over the campus about the events at Lawrence House and Rosemary found herself a minor celebrity. Fern had been taken out of school by her shocked parents, a pair who looked as old-fashioned and strait-laced as she, and was put under the care of a psychiatrist. Surprisingly, not even Beverly wanted to press charges. The jeweler returned Nancy's bracelet after he had been reimbursed by the Watermans. Beverly's pen and pencil set was found among Fern's things. Her parents also made restitution to Lee Ann for the fifty dollars Fern had stolen. It turned out that Fern really hadn't needed money at all, for her parents were well-to-do. Her mother confessed to Mr. Lawrence that Fern had been in difficulty once in high school over the same thing, but they had not thought it serious enough to seek psychiatric treatment for her.

By the end of the week life at Lawrence House resumed its normal pace and even Wilma stopped talking continually about Fern, although she still seemed lost without her dominating roommate.

Rosemary had been driven back to the house on several occasions recently by Thad. On one occasion he wanted to show her Alicia's pearl ring after it was finished. She exclaimed over its simple beauty.

"You think Alicia will like it, then?" he asked boyishly.

"If she doesn't, she's a very foolish girl," Rosemary said. "And we know that isn't so."

Thad himself had become a celebrity also. The debate squad had won first place at the Manchester Tournament, winning all twelve of its debates against top competition from all over the country. Thad received a major portion of the credit as being the only senior member of the squad and also debate chairman. The squad's picture was adorning the May issue of the alumni magazine.

Esther and Rosemary were getting ready for supper that night when Esther turned to Rosemary with a rather serious expression. "There's something I ought to tell you," she said hesitatingly. "I hope you'll take it in the spirit it's intended."

Rosemary whirled from the mirror and stared at her roommate. "All right, out with it," she said. "Have I done something wrong again?"

"It's about Thad Thompson," Esther said, her face scarlet. "The girls are talking about your being seen with him so much."

"The girls or Beverly Coleman?" Rosemary snapped, rather nettled.

Esther nodded. "I think Beverly started the talk, Rosemary. But everyone thinks it's . . . well, rather strange, when you and Alicia have been such good friends and then you're riding with her boy friend all the time."

Rosemary shrugged. "There isn't anything to it, Esther, you know that. Thad's just been nice to me and . . . well,

I enjoy being with him. In fact, he likes to talk about Alicia to me." She frowned. "Has Alicia said anything?"

Esther shook her head. "You know Alicia. She wouldn't say anything if her heart were broken. And then you haven't been seeing Gray lately, either. Naturally, everybody's gossiping. You know how girls are."

The supper bell rang. Rosemary said, "Thanks, Esther, for telling me." At supper she made a special point to talk to Alicia, and Alicia, good sport that she was, acted as though nothing at all was wrong, although her smile seemed slightly strained.

That night, in bed, Rosemary resolved to make up with Gray and then the gossip would stop. After all, Thad had Alicia's ring now and the debate season was over, so there was really nothing for him to see her about any longer, anyway.

There was just the faintest tinge of regret as she turned over and smoothed her pillow. Thad had been fun and she had enjoyed the occasions with him. He had been a new experience for her. But there would never be anything further for her with a boy like Thad, so she might as well face it and remember that he was in love with one of her best friends. He would tell Alicia when he gave her the ring about Rosemary's part in it, she was sure, and Alicia would understand then.

"How would you like to try out for the debate team next year, Miss Rossiter?" Professor Hayworth asked Rosemary the next day after public-speaking class. "We'll be losing Thad, and I'd like to have one girl on the team anyway." The team had been all masculine this season.

Rosemary was flattered by the invitation. "I'd love to, Professor Hayworth, if I come back to Waverly."

"You come back, young lady. I have my eye on you for our department, you know," he said in a jocular manner.

As she turned to leave, Rosemary saw Gray waiting uncertainly by the door. She took her courage in hand and walked straight up to him. "Hello, Gray," she said lightly. "Long time no see."

His eyes were steady on hers. "Hello, Rosemary. You've been so busy I didn't think you'd even notice my absence."

"I've been busy but not the way you think, Gray," she said, deciding to be completely honest. "I've missed seeing you a great deal." Automatically, they turned and walked down the corridor together, as they used to do after class.

He looked at Rosemary as though he wanted to believe her. "And Thad Thompson? You're not going steady with him?"

Rosemary laughed, a bright, relaxed peal of laughter. "Oh, Gray, where did you get that crazy idea? Thad and I are just good friends. He's in love with Alicia. I thought you knew that."

But Gray persisted doggedly. "Beverly told me you were dating. She said you two were seeing each other all the time now."

"Why, that cat!" Rosemary cried, stopping dead in her tracks. "You should know better than to believe anything she says, Gray."

Gray's eyes immediately took on their old roguish twinkle, and he looked the jaunty self Rosemary liked so much. He grabbed her arm. "Come on, then, let's go over to Howley's and celebrate!" He pulled her along while she was gasping, "What . . . are we . . . celebrating, Gray?"

"That it's a spring day and you're my girl again and . . . well, isn't that enough?" he shouted, beaming down at her.

She was almost running beside him now. "That's enough, Gray." It was so wonderful being with him again. Had any spring day ever been so bright and gay before?

As they reached the back door of Howley's, he pulled her over behind the lilac bush which was laden with purple bloom. "Dear little Rosemary," he murmured, and kissed her for the first time.

She knew that never again would she ever take Gray lightly, and that, as long as she lived, lilacs would remind her of that day.

Early Saturday morning Esther left for Echo Lake with Tony. She would pick him up in town, as usual, to escape detection, she told her roommate. From the upstairs window Rosemary watched Esther pull away from the curb in her blue convertible. Why doesn't she tell her parents? Rosemary thought, as she had so many times before. But Esther remained adamant. Her parents were still talking about sending her to a school in the East next year. It all seems so pointless, Rosemary thought, because they've got to find out sometime.

Rosemary walked over to observe at the speech clinic this morning. She found the waiting room packed and the one assistant looking harried. Professor Hayworth was inside the glass-walled cubicle making an examination of a little girl. He smiled through the window at Rosemary and stuck his head out of the door. "Care to give us a hand, Miss

Rossiter?" he asked. "One of the assistants is ill this morning."

"I'd be happy to, sir," Rosemary said, glad of the opportunity to be of service. "What can I do?"

"Could you fill out clinic cards on the children waiting?"

"Surely." Rosemary hung her coat on the hall tree. Professor Hayworth seated her at the desk in the waiting room and handed her a printed 3 x 5 card. "Just get the requested information on each child. Be careful to spell the names correctly and keep them in order. You shouldn't have any trouble, Miss Rossiter."

He hurried back inside where the little girl was already trying to run the wire recorder. "You see, Miss Rossiter, you can't leave them alone long," he said over his shoulder, seizing the child's hands just as she started winding them in the wire.

Rosemary looked around the room. Saturday was always the busiest day at the clinic. "Who's next?" she asked politely.

A fat, dowdily dressed woman with a cross expression jerked a small wan-looking boy forward. "I am!" She snapped. "I've been waiting a half-hour. The service here is terrible!"

Rosemary pointed to the chair by the desk. "Please sit down, madam," she said, ignoring the woman's complaint. "What is the child's name?" The little boy looked none too happy, so Rosemary smiled at him and patted his head.

"Billy Murphy," his mother replied.

"Age?"

"Six."

Rosemary got the address, telephone number, parents' name, school, and other necessary information, printing it clearly. "What is the nature of the child's speech defect?" she asked.

Billy ducked his head and looked embarrassed. "Why, he stammers a little, but kids outgrow that," his mother said. "It ain't nothing to worry about. I wouldn't of even brung him, except his teacher kept insisting. Teachers has got a lot of crazy ideas nowadays."

Rosemary recognized at once that Mrs. Murphy was not going to be a cooperative parent. She spoke to Billy gently. "Do you like to go to school, Billy?"

Billy gulped and nodded. "I—It's O—O K—K," he replied. "I—I c—can't t—talk s—so g—good, th—though. T—The k—kids all laugh a—at m—me." His eyes filled with tears, and he rubbed his eyes.

Rosemary felt pity for the unhappy-looking child. "I'm sure Professor Hayworth can help you, Billy, if you just do what he says."

He began sniffling and looked guiltily at his mother. Mrs. Murphy sniffed. She stood up and glared at Rosemary. "I'm not goin' to wait much longer. This is a lot of foolishness anyway." Billy was still crying. "For heaven's sake, stop that blubbering!" she screeched at him. "There ain't a blessed thing to cry about!"

Rosemary had to bite her lip to keep from telling Mrs. Murphy what she thought of her, and turned her eyes away from the unfortunate Billy. It was too bad the parents couldn't have some kind of treatment, too. It was no wonder the child had a speech defect with a mother like that.

"Next, please," she said. There were eight patients, two with cleft palates, a partly deaf child, and five stammerers. By the time she had interviewed all of them, Rosemary was growing weary. Some parents were uncooperative, like Mrs. Murphy. Others were anxious; some were indifferent, as Professor Hayworth had mentioned in his lectures to the class.

Two of the children had been brought over from the Waverly Orphans' Home by an attendant. From the sight of their wistful, love-starved eyes, Rosemary concluded that the main solution to their speech problem would be a liberal dose of attention and affection.

Through the glass window she could see Professor Hayworth and his assistant testing, examining, and training. She stayed until the last little patient had been taken in, one of the orphans. Then Professor Hayworth stuck his head out. "You can run along now, Miss Rossiter. The clinic closes at noon and it's almost that now. Thanks for your impromptu help."

"All right, sir," she said. "Just call on me any time you're short-handed."

He smiled and closed the door. Rosemary put on her coat and went out into the balmy spring sunshine. Tiny leaflets were popping out on the trees, and the turf was a luscious green. It's just three weeks, she thought, until Mother's wedding. And then she'll be gone. Aunt Caroline said I could stay with them this summer if I wanted to work in Farmingdale. Should I do that or should I go on out to Iowa?

As she came up to Lawrence House, Rosemary noticed a shiny new Lincoln parked at the curb. One of the girls must have company for lunch, she thought. Probably Beverly's father with an expensive car like that.

As she went past Mr. Lawrence's office, Rosemary saw him in conversation with a middle-aged couple. The man looked like a successful business executive; the petite, well-dressed woman was blond and pretty. A warning bell rang in Rosemary's brain just as Irving Lawrence turned and saw her.

"Miss Rossiter, will you step in here a moment?" he called. Rosemary wished she could vanish into thin air, but she had no choice but to respond.

The man rose when she entered. "These are Esther's parents, Miss Rossiter," Mr. Lawrence said. "They came to surprise Esther and take her home for the weekend."

Mrs. Mercer, who looked amazingly like Esther, was looking dismayed. "Hello, Rosemary," she said. "It's so nice to meet you at last in person." Her voice quickened. "But we can't understand about Esther. Mr. Lawrence says she signed out this morning and said she was going home. We called home to see if we had passed each other on the road and the maid said Esther has never arrived."

Rosemary felt the three pairs of anxious eyes fasten on her. "Perhaps she stopped to . . . to eat somewhere," she said in a weak voice. It was all she could think of to say on the spur of the moment.

Mr. Mercer shook his head. "She wouldn't do that," he said brusquely. "Mr. Lawrence said Esther left at eight o'clock. It's only eighty-five miles. She'd be home in time for lunch." He had an important, booming voice, as though he were used to issuing orders.

Mr. Lawrence spoke thoughtfully. "Surely she should be

in Freesburg by now. Esther is a fine driver and keeps her car in excellent condition. It's most peculiar, most peculiar, to be sure." He looked at Rosemary reproachfully, as though she should be able to supply the answer.

Rosemary wished she could crawl under the rug, for Mrs. Mercer began to cry. "I just know something's happened to Esther," she sobbed. "She's such a timid little thing. She wouldn't know what to do in an emergency."

Mr. Mercer cleared his throat. "Perhaps we'd better call the police," he said worriedly. He patted his wife's shoulder. "Now just calm down, dear. No use jumping to conclusions yet."

Rosemary was battling valiantly with her conscience. She had promised Esther faithfully to keep her secret, but was it right to let her parents suffer this way? And if they called the police, they would certainly find out the truth soon enough. For a frantic instant Rosemary debated with herself, for Mr. Mercer had picked up the telephone and Mrs. Mercer was still weeping into her white linen handkerchief.

Rosemary took a deep breath and braced herself. "I know where Esther is," she said.

Mr. Mercer slowly put down the telephone and Mrs. Mercer looked up in surprise. There was a moment of shocked silence before Rosemary said, "She's at Echo Lake."

"Echo Lake?" Mr. Mercer echoed, as though he didn't believe her. "What in heaven's name is she doing there?"

Irving Lawrence was looking at Rosemary as though he, too, doubted her sanity. Echo Lake was a well-known sum-

mer resort, but the season would not open for at least a
month.

Only Mrs. Mercer looked as though she believed her.
She put down her handkerchief. "I knew it," she said in
a hopeless tone. "It's that Tony Risotti, isn't it, Rosemary?"

"Yes, ma'am, it is. But it isn't what you think," Rosemary
added quickly, seeing the distressed look the Mercers exchanged. "They're . . . well, they're married. They got married last August, in fact. They're staying at Tony's parents'
cabin there."

The Mercers looked as though they were frozen. Irving
Lawrence opened his mouth and then closed it again. It was
Mr. Mercer who finally spoke. "Are you completely sure,
Rosemary? This isn't a joke of some kind?"

"Yes, sir, I'm sure. Esther told me herself some time
ago. She made me promise not to tell anyone. I'm very
sorry I had to break my promise to her."

Mrs. Mercer was murmuring, "Married! Whatever possessed her?" She looked completely bewildered.

Rosemary decided she might as well tell the whole
truth, since she had already begun. "They were sure you'd
never approve, so they eloped," she said. But she couldn't
help feeling sorry for Esther's parents, because they looked
so stunned.

Mr. Mercer blew his nose loudly. He had lost his self-
assured manner. "Our little girl—married? It just doesn't
seem possible."

Irving Lawrence, who had not said a word until now, said
quietly, "Perhaps you'd better go now, Miss Rossiter.
Thank you for your help."

"Yes, thank you, Rosemary. You were brave to tell us against Esther's wishes," Mrs. Mercer said. Mr. Mercer echoed her thanks. When Rosemary left, he was bending over his wife solicitously.

Rosemary felt half-ashamed, half-relieved. Esther would probably be furious with her, but she had really had no choice. Esther had been wrong in not telling her parents long ago.

She realized she had not had any lunch yet. The other girls were gathered in the lounge. As usual, when something was going on of importance, the girls had gotten the word and were conjecturing about what was transpiring in Mr. Lawrence's office. They tried to pump Rosemary, but she would say nothing.

When the lunch bell sounded, the office door was still closed. After lunch, Rosemary saw the Mercers driving away in their big car. Mr. Lawrence did not say any more about the matter to Rosemary and it was as though nothing had occurred.

Thus she was astounded when a beaming Esther came into their room on Sunday evening. Before she even took off her coat she ran over to Rosemary and threw her arms around her.

"You darling!" she said. "How can I ever repay you?"

Rosemary drew back and stared dazedly at her roommate. "You're not mad at me?"

Esther tossed her coat on her bed. "Mad? Of course not, silly. I owe everything to you. I'm deliriously happy!"

Rosemary could not have been more surprised. She had been dreading Esther's return and had been thinking of how she was ever going to explain her treachery to her roommate.

Esther threw herself down in her chair. "Mother and Dad came up to Echo Lake yesterday after they'd been here. They insisted we both go home with them. At first I didn't want to, but Tony made me. He said we might as well face the music, that we had been putting it off too long." She looked rather sheepish. "They were so nice, Rosemary, not at all as I thought they'd be. They said they were disappointed that we had eloped, but now that we were married, they intended to make the best of it. They want us to get a little apartment and live together until we finish school. They're going to help us financially. Isn't that wonderful, Rosemary?" Esther had not looked so happy for a long time.

Rosemary was so relieved she felt like whooping for joy. "I'm so glad, Esther. I felt so bad about having to tell your folks, but it's all worked out for the best."

Esther smiled mischievously. "Now they're all excited, hoping there'll be a grandchild before too long. They're really being swell, Rosemary. And we even all drove over to Tony's folks today and told them. They were nice about it, too. We all had a good visit and got acquainted."

Rosemary said, "I wish you'd tell the other girls you're married, Esther. They're all dying to know what's been going on ever since your folks were here yesterday."

"Don't worry, Rosemary. I want to shout it from the housetops now." She went out into the hall, and Rosemary heard her going from room to room telling the glad news.

Rosemary walked to the window and stared out over the campus. It was just growing dark, and the pink dogwood and red azaleas made bright dashes of color in the gray of the evening. She was glad she had been of help to Esther, but she was sorry she would be losing a good roommate. It seemed as though, one by one, she always lost everyone she loved.

CHAPTER 13

May Wedding

THE MORNING OF FRANCES ROSSITER'S WEDDING DAWNED
bright and clear, a perfect May day. Gray had borrowed a
car and was driving Rosemary to Farmingdale after breakfast. The wedding was scheduled for two thirty and they
would drive back to Waverly after the honeymooners had
left.

Rosemary packed the new dress she had bought for the
event at her mother's insistence. Jesse had sent her the
money, a gift from her new father-to-be, he had written.
Rosemary had selected a light blue chiffon which would
make a good date dress during the summer—if she had any
dates! Her mother was wearing pink and Aunt Caroline,
lavender, so the blue would blend well with the other colors.

Esther had already left with Tony to look for apartments
in Waverly. As soon as the semester ended, they would be
moving out of their respective houses and into their new
home. Esther had been ecstatically happy lately. Rosemary
wished, with a little envy, that her own future was as
assured. She seemed to be good at helping other people
solve their problems but couldn't work out her own.

Cynthia was proudly sporting a fraternity pin from her
stepmother's cousin at Ohio State. Fern was in a private

sanitarium undergoing psychiatric treatment. Her mother had written Mr. Lawrence that they were hoping Fern would be well enough to re-enter Waverly in the fall. Alicia and Thad were absorbed in each other and making plans for their future together. It seemed as though everyone had something to look forward to but herself, Rosemary thought, indulging in a moment of self-pity.

But she shook herself briskly and snapped the lock on her weekend case, because it was time for Gray to arrive. She walked downstairs and signed out. Gray was as punctual as usual, punctuality being one of his virtues, Rosemary had found. His spirits were high, and in spite of herself Rosemary began to enjoy the day and the prospect of seeing her family again.

"It doesn't seem possible school is almost out," Gray commented as they rode along the countryside fragrant with the scent of apple trees in blossom.

"I know it, Gray," Rosemary said, sighing. "It seems only yesterday I came to Waverly. What day are you starting with Dr. Fosdick?"

"Just as soon as classses are over. Have you made up your mind what you're going to do yet, Rosemary?" His gray eyes were concerned as they rested on her profile.

Rosemary shook her head. "Aunt Caroline and Uncle Leon have invited me to stay with them. But they're out in the country off the bus line, so that would mean Uncle Leon would have to drive me into Farmingdale, if I got a job there. Mother's already put our house in the hands of a real-estate agent, so I can't stay there. I could go out to Iowa, but I hate to intrude on Mother and Jesse right away." She spread her hands out in a helpless gesture.

"So-o-o, I honestly don't know, Gray. I feel at such loose ends."

He nodded sympathetically. "You do have a problem, I can see that, Rosemary. But I'd think the best solution would be to go on out to Iowa with your mother."

Rosemary didn't answer, for it was partly the idea of going so far away from Gray that held her back. But she could not very well tell him that.

When they reached Farmingdale, it was only noon, so they drove directly to Rosemary's home. It was the last time that she'd be coming there, Rosemary thought sadly, the home she had been born in. Her mother, looking excited and happy, greeted them at the door.

"So this is Gray Horton," she said, taking his hand and looking at him appraisingly. "I was beginning to think we were never going to meet."

"So did I, Mrs. Rossiter," he said, smiling. "It must have been a conspiracy to keep us apart." Rosemary felt proud of him. He looked so nice in his dark-blue suit and white shirt. She could tell that her mother liked him and that Gray liked her.

"Well, do come in," Frances said, drawing them into the living room. "Everything's all set, Rosemary. The moving men are coming in Monday and moving everything. The agent thinks he has a buyer for the house. Jesse and I will be renting in Fremont for a while. The superintendent of schools has a house all lined up for us."

Rosemary looked around the living room. Already it had a strange appearance with the familiar knickknacks and pictures put away. It was already not the home she remembered.

"Have you had any lunch?" Frances was asking. "I made a bowl of potato salad and some sandwiches in case you hadn't eaten."

"No, we haven't eaten, Mother. We thought we'd better come directly here."

"That sounds good," Gray said. "Rosemary and I can do up the dishes while you get ready, Mrs. Rossiter. Doing dishes is my specialty."

So the three of them sat down in the kitchen, although Frances was too excited to eat very much. She looks like a girl today, Rosemary thought. Her eyes were unclouded and her skin glowing.

Her mother asked Gray about his college classes, about the veterinary program, and in her inimitable way of extracting information without seeming to, soon knew everything about him. Gray chatted easily with her, told her about his own parents and their farm, his summer job, and even about the night he and Rosemary had met at Lawrence House. Rosemary sat back and enjoyed letting them get acquainted.

Before they realized it, the time had passed and it was time for Frances to get ready for the wedding. While Gray and Rosemary straightened up the kitchen, Frances put on the pink silk suit, the pink pumps dyed to match, and the petal-covered pink hat with the tiny back veil. Jesse had sent her a nosegay of purple violets and pink sweet peas to carry.

When Rosemary came into her mother's bedroom, Frances was standing before the mirror, looking at herself in her wedding finery. Rosemary put her arms around her and hugged her.

"You're so pretty, Mother, and I'm so proud of you," she said mistily. "I hope you're very happy."

Frances patted Rosemary's shoulder and they were silent for an emotional moment. Then she drew back and looked into her daughter's eyes. "I hope you're going to love Jesse, too, dear," she said softly. "I know no one will ever take your father's place." She looked sad for a moment. "But Jesse is a good man, too." She smiled brightly then, gave Rosemary a little spank, and exclaimed, "Go get dressed or you're going to miss the wedding!"

The moment was gone, never to be recovered, and Rosemary knew in a moment of truth that things would never be exactly the same again between them.

Rosemary changed into her new blue chiffon dress. Jesse had sent her a nosegay of Talisman roses. She put on the perky little half-hat which just matched the blue dress, hastily applied a cherry-red lipstick, and she was ready, too.

Gray whistled when she came out to the kitchen. "Wow! You look like a bride yourself! How about making it a double wedding?" He dropped a quick kiss on her cheek, and she felt immeasurably happy, even though she knew he was only joking.

Leon and Caroline arrived, Caroline looking regal and statuesque in her lavender lace dress and floppy brimmed hat. They met Gray, there were hurried greetings all around, and in a moment Leon and Caroline had driven off to the church with Frances. Gray and Rosemary followed in the borrowed car.

The simple but impressive ceremony took only a few moments. Rosemary watched Jesse standing at the altar rail beside her mother, looking so distinguished in his dark-blue suit, his head slightly bent as he listened to the age-old words. When the minister said, "For better, for worse, for richer, for poorer," Gray took Rosemary's hand and she had to swallow to keep from bursting into tears. She tried to control herself by thinking of something else.

Traffic sounds were muted in the distance, and somewhere a dog was barking, while the minister's wife played softly on the old organ, "I Loveth Thee." Why did women always want to cry at weddings? Rosemary thought. It was really so silly.

How sunburned Uncle Leon looks, Rosemary thought irrelevantly, still trying to control her emotions. He's sturdier looking than Jesse, she decided, but not quite so good-looking. Aunt Caroline never changes. She always looks so calm and serene. She looks like a page out of *Vogue* rather than a farmer's wife who gets out in the fields and runs the tractor. I hope I age as well as she and Mother have. Why, Mother's almost forty, and Aunt Caroline's past forty. They're getting old and they're still pretty.

Gray was still holding Rosemary's hand. It made her feel so secure, so peaceful. Somehow having Gray there with her helped assuage the sense of loss she felt, for her mother never again would be wholly hers.

Suddenly the ceremony was over and everyone was laughing and kissing the bride. Jesse came over to Rosemary at once. He smiled down at her, his eyes gentle. "Hello, Rosemary. I don't expect you to call me Dad right away, because I know how you felt about your own father, but let's start out being friends. Why don't you just call me Jesse?"

"All right, Jesse," Rosemary said simply. She put out her hand, and they shook hands solemnly. There was a quality about him that reminded her of Gray, a certain inner strength that shone in their eyes.

Uncle Leon was passing out rice, so Jesse and Frances ran out to their car in a shower of rice. They waved good-by and then they were gone. Gray took Rosemary's arm. She was still staring after them blindly, although the car had turned the corner and was out of sight. "Come on, Rosemary," he said softly. "Let's go back and pick up your bag and be on our way to Waverly."

Uncle Leon would handle the final negotiations about the house and the moving. There was nothing left for Rosemary but to pick up her bag and lock the door on yesterday. She knew that this was going to be the most difficult part of all.

CHAPTER 14

Awards Day

ONE AFTERNOON THE FOLLOWING WEEK ALICIA CAME DASH-
ing into Rosemary's room. The efficient Alicia was busier
than ever now that graduation was approaching. She hesitated inside the door. "I just wanted you to know Michael's
last lesson is tomorrow, Rosemary. He's improved enough
to be discharged from the clinic."

"Oh, Alicia, I'm so glad! You must be terribly proud of
the job you've done with him," Rosemary replied. She was
slaving over her own term paper for botany.

Alicia nodded. "It is gratifying, Rosemary. Michael's talking plainly even if slowly. His folks are so grateful to the
clinic." It was typical of Alicia's modesty that she did not
say "grateful to me."

Rosemary's eyes went to Alicia's left hand. Evidently
Thad had not yet given her the pearl ring, for she was sure
Alicia would be wearing it if she had received it.

"Are you and Beverly on speaking terms again?" she asked,
her brown eyes dancing.

"Oh, my, yes! Beverly never stays mad long," Alicia replied. "She gave up on Thad after the Valentine Dance.
I guess she saw it was hopeless that night."

Rosemary grinned. "It's a good thing, Alicia. Beverly

might as well learn to accept the inevitable. She can't have everything she wants just for the asking." Beverly had been cool to her ever since the day she had caught Rosemary looking at Alicia's ring. Rosemary had never forgiven her, either, for telling Gray that Thad and Rosemary were dating, and for trying to cause hard feelings between her and Alicia. Alicia had never alluded to the matter, and the slight strain between her and Rosemary was gone.

Alicia glanced at her watch. "I've got to run, Rosemary. I have to get measured for my cap and gown. By for now."

Rosemary had written only one more paragraph on the function of stamens when Nancy stuck her red head in the door. "How about a coke, Rosemary?" she suggested.

Rosemary sighed. "I oughtn't to, Nancy. This paper's due Wednesday and I'm only half finished."

"Oh, come on, drudge!" Nancy urged. "Do you good to get out a little. How can you stick in this old dark room on such a nice day?"

It was, indeed, a nice day, so Rosemary ignored her conscience and went over to Howley's with Nancy. The hangout was virtually deserted, for the campus was dotted with couples sitting on the lawn or strolling along the canal path through the woods. The flower bed around Samuel Waverly's statue was ablaze now with red- and yellow-striped tulips.

The girls sipped their cokes silently. It was pleasant to relax for a few moments, after all, Rosemary decided. The past couple of weeks had been such hectic ones—her mother's wedding, preparing term papers, studying for finals. Uncle Leon had written Rosemary that the Rossiter house had been sold and he had supervised the moving of the household goods. Her mother had written several ecstatic notes from Canada, and the last had said they would soon be on their way to Iowa.

Rosemary realized that Nancy was telling about her summer project of working at a children's camp. She would be leaving the day after school was out for a northern lake. Rosemary listened enviously. Everybody had interesting plans but herself, it seemed. The summer stretched ahead as an empty void. Gray would be busy with his assistanceship. Rosemary couldn't hope to see much of him. Listening to Nancy's plans, she sighed unconsciously. Nancy looked at her with quick understanding, for with her keen perception she could always sense what was in Rosemary's mind.

"Have you ever thought of asking Mr. Lawrence if you could stay at the house this summer, Rosemary?" she asked. "Maybe you could find something to do here in Waverly."

Rosemary looked at her friend with sudden interest. "You know, I never even thought of that, Nancy," she said. "I naturally assumed the house would be closed."

Nancy shook her head. "Mr. Lawrence never leaves the place and Nellie is here year round, too. And even though there aren't any summer classes, the college offices stay open all summer. If there isn't anything doing at the college, there might be something in town."

Rosemary hurriedly finished her coke. "I'm going right back and ask Mr. Lawrence. Thanks for suggesting it, Nancy." She had the germ of an idea which just might work out.

Rosemary found Mr. Lawrence in his office. He listened courteously while she explained her predicament. He said slowly, "During the summer we renovate the rooms and get things in shape for fall, Miss Rossiter. But I suppose one girl in the house wouldn't make too much difference. Nellie has to cook for me anyway." He paused, and smiled at her. "I could let you stay in your room if you wish. After all, Miss Rossiter, I do owe you something for clearing up the mystery of the thefts. That was a great relief to me, a very great relief."

Rosemary could have hugged him. Now if only the second part of her idea worked out, she would have her summer plans made finally. She thanked Mr. Lawrence profusely and hurried across the campus.

Professor Hayworth was just coming out of the speech clinic when Rosemary came in, panting from her rapid pace. He smiled when he saw her. "Ah, Miss Rossiter, you're a trifle late today. I just saw our last case."

"I wanted to talk with you about something personal, sir."

He lifted his eyebrows. "Sit down and let's talk, then. What did you have on your mind, Miss Rossiter?"

Now that she was facing him, Rosemary felt timid about asking. "I was wondering, sir, if you could use an assistant in the clinic this summer. I can type and take shorthand. I'd be willing to do anything, though. You see, I've decided definitely to become a speech correctionist."

Professor Hayworth looked pleased, but then he frowned. "I'm glad to hear that, Rosemary. The trouble is—we don't function during the summer in the department. In fact, I'm going up to the University of Wisconsin myself to teach this summer. I'm leaving the day after classes are over here."

Rosemary's face fell. She had counted so on Professor

Hayworth's being able to use her. Her disappointment was almost a sickness within her.

"I'm sorry. I wish I could help you. Have you applied for a scholarship?"

"No, sir," she replied. "But even if I got a scholarship for next year, I'd still have to find something for the summer." Rosemary couldn't tell him the intimate fact that she couldn't sponge off her new stepfather for the summer.

She rose. "I won't take any more of your time, sir," she said. "It was just an idea."

Professor Hayworth walked to the door with her. "We'll be looking forward to your assisting in the clinic next year, then, Miss Rossiter."

She nodded, said thank you, and went out into the sunshine. Darn it! she thought. Why can't anything ever work out the way I want it to? She felt low enough to eat the tulips which were blooming along the walks.

In a few days Rosemary had a long letter from her mother detailing the many attractions of Fremont, and begging Rosemary to come out as soon as school was over. She and Jesse would send Rosemary the train fare if she would come. It was a busy little town and she was positive Rosemary could find a summer job. She was divinely happy and loved her new home, although she missed Rosemary and Leon and Caroline.

In the same mail was a letter from Aunt Caroline, asking Rosemary if she had decided to come stay with them for the summer. They would love to have her "to brighten up their lonely old age," as she put it. Rosemary smiled, thinking of her energetic, youthful aunt and uncle. They were anything but old. Well, she had two offers, at least. And there still was the promise from Mr. Lawrence to let her stay in her room. Gray would be only fifty miles away then during the vacation months.

Friday was Awards Day, and the entire student body would attend the convocation. As was the custom, the Lawrence girls would attend and sit in a body as would the residents of the other houses. There was always a great deal of good-natured rivalry among the houses over the awards. The big event of the day would be the new Good Citizenship award.

Rosemary listened with divided attention at the breakfast table as the other girls talked of the convocation.

"It's all sort of silly, I think," Beverly said, shrugging her shapely shoulders. "After all, who cares who's the best citizen? It's like grammar school—who's going to be class monitor?"

Lee Ann spoke up with a vigor she rarely expressed. "It's a fine, worth-while contest, Beverly, and it will be an honor if someone from our house wins. After all, what's more valuable to a person than being able to get along well with others?" Her remark was so pointed and fitting that several of the girls openly snickered. Beverly tossed her head and quickly asked for the orange marmalade.

Rosemary walked to the auditorium between Nancy and Esther. Esther was so ecstatic over the little apartment she and Tony had finally found that she could talk of nothing else. Rosemary had already lost her roommate in spirit if not in body. Esther's conversation now was of choosing drapery material, whether her bedroom furniture would fit into the tiny bedroom, of Tony's interesting family, and her collection of recipes. Her school life was secondary to Esther now. She was first of all a wife, then a student, Rosemary thought.

The Lawrence girls had decided to wear blue skirts and white blouses, so they presented a trim, uniform appearance. They found seats together near the front of the auditorium.

Rosemary found herself seated between Alicia and Beverly. She tried to think of something to say to Beverly but it was always hard for her to converse with the older girl. "What are you going to do when school is out, Beverly?" she finally asked, trying hard to be friendly, and letting bygones be bygones.

"We'll be taking a cruise probably on Father's yacht," she replied in a superior way, "or go up to our summer home in the Adirondacks. It'll be a perfectly mad season, so many places to go, and so little time." She pouted prettily. "I do wish Father would let me change schools next year, though. Just because Mother went to Waverly, he insists I get my degree here, too. It's so . . . well, you know, Middle Westerny."

"Yes, I suppose it is, Beverly," Rosemary said lamely. "But I like it here very much."

Beverly's patronizing expression said, "You would, you peasant!" She turned her head to smile at a boy in the next row.

Alicia nudged Rosemary. "There's Gray looking over this way." She pointed him out to Rosemary where he sat with the boys from his house. He grinned at Rosemary from across the auditorium.

The dean rapped for attention, and the convocation was under way. The athletic awards were handed out first; then the scholastic awards to the seniors. Both Alicia and Thad received awards in their respective departments, and Rosemary felt a thrill of pride in her friends' success. They made such a handsome couple on the platform.

Next the underclassmen awards for scholastic achievement were granted. Rosemary was not at all surprised that she did not receive any recognition here. Donna Farrell from Lawrence House had the highest average in the freshman class with a straight-A average. The Lawrence girls applauded when Donna went forward for her award.

"The poor thing's such a drip! It's a good thing she has brains, at least," Beverly whispered. Rosemary thought the remark exceedingly unkind and did not deign to reply. She liked Donna even though they had not become close friends, for Donna was so engrossed in her studies that she was not on intimate terms with anyone.

Nancy Potter received an award for being the outstanding freshman student in chemistry. It was always surprising to everyone that the jolly Nancy was such a good student. Alicia whispered to Rosemary, "Lawrence House is coming off with a lot of awards as usual. No wonder Mr. Lawrence is always so proud of his girls."

Rosemary nodded and wished she could have done something to add to the honor of the house. She was always so dismally average in everything. But she squared her shoulders and applauded without envy when Nancy stepped forward for her honor. The proscenium lights glinted on her red hair, and she was striking enough to provoke some wolf whistles from the balcony. Nancy grinned good-humoredly and tossed a kiss upward toward the balcony. Even the dignified dean had to smile. Nancy could wring a smile out of a turnip, Rosemary thought.

The dean harrumphed, adjusted his nose glasses, and looked mysterious. "Now comes the award you all have been waiting for, the Good Citizenship award." A rustle of anticipation went over the audience. "May I present Professor Hayworth, chairman of the faculty committee which made the final decision?"

Professor Hayworth stepped forward, his small body erect as always. "An anonymous donor who has been impressed with Waverly College and its students has set up a trust fund to provide this award annually," he said. "The award in the case of a senior is five hundred dollars cash. For an underclassman, it will be one year's free tuition at the college."

A wild burst of applause broke out. Professor Hayworth held up his hand. "Please, students. Hold your applause for the winners. In addition, the house whose candidate wins the honor will receive some useful appliance. This year it will be a color television set."

"My goodness!" Beverly whispered, for once as excited as everyone else. "The donor must be someone with a lot of money."

Professor Hayworth was consulting his notes. "First, the male winner. This boy is well known on the campus. He has contributed much to Waverly College and has engaged in many worth-while activities throughout his college career. His outstanding contribution this year was his unceasing effort as chairman of debate to build a winning varsity squad which has brought national honor and recognition to Waverly. This senior is Thaddeus Thompson."

Alicia gasped audibly, and Rosemary put her hand over Alicia's. "That's wonderful, Alicia," she said. The students were showing their wholehearted approval by clapping, whistling, and stomping. Alicia looked almost overcome with pride.

Beverly swallowed visibly and leaned across Rosemary. "Congrats, Alicia," she said in a brittle voice. "You must be terribly proud of Thad."

Alicia nodded, her eyes shining. "Yes, I am, Beverly, very proud." Rosemary was hoping Alicia would win the girls' award. That would be perfect for the two of them, and no one deserved it more than Alicia.

Professor Hayworth was rapping for attention. "The feminine winner had the unique honor of being nominated by every member of her house save two—and we naturally assume one of those was her own vote!" Everyone laughed. "She is not only liked by her housemates but was even voted for by the house director. And that is unusual." Another laugh. "I know this student well. She is going to be very much surprised that she is held in such high esteem by her friends, because she thinks of herself as completely average. May I quote from her nomination letter, 'Not only has she unselfishly given of herself to her housemates, but singlehanded she solved a series of robberies which had been plaguing her house.' Our winner is a first-semester freshman, Rosemary Rossiter."

When Rosemary heard her name pronounced, she sat unbelieving, staring blankly at Professor Hayworth. Surely there must be some mistake. She hadn't done anything at all except to catch Fern and she still felt sorry about that.

Then she realized that Alicia was urging her to get up.

Numbly, as though she were someone else and she was sitting in her seat watching, Rosemary made her way through the aisle, each Lawrence girl but Beverly saying a congratulatory word as she passed. She walked with rubbery legs to the platform where Professor Hayworth shook her hand warmly. He said, under cover of the applause, "Do you realize this means you'll be coming back to Waverly, Rosemary?"

She looked up into his kindly eyes, trying to grasp his meaning. Why, of course, a year's free tuition! Her next year was assured. She said humbly, "Thank you, sir," and took the envelope from his hand. Inside was a certificate that could be framed.

By the time she reached her seat, Rosemary was trembling all over. Why did you become so tingly inside when something like this happened? she thought. Everyone was talking and shaking her hand. But what she was most aware of was Gray coming to her through the crowd. When he finally reached her he said simply, "And to think, Rosemary Rossiter, you're my girl!" He looked as though he would like to kiss her, but he contented himself with just looking at her with his heart in his eyes.

CHAPTER 15

Till September

THE COLOR TELEVISION WAS DELIVERED TO LAWRENCE HOUSE on the Monday following Awards Day. Mr. Lawrence was so proud of his house's winning so many honors that they were treated with a turkey dinner and all the trimmings that night, plus Nellie's angel-food cake which was her contribution to the occasion.

The dazed Rosemary still could hardly realize what had happened. From being the lowliest person in the house, a first-semester freshman and a poor one at that, she had suddenly been catapulted into a position of prominence. Everybody on the campus spoke to her now. Boys who had never noticed her before had already called for dates. These she refused with graciousness. After all, she was Gray Horton's girl and her winning the award hadn't changed that at all. Gray had liked her when she was a complete nonentity.

Rosemary and Esther went upstairs, full of turkey and dressing. They sprawled on their beds for a few moments before starting to the library for some last-minute reference work. Tomorrow was the beginning of finals—four days of exams and then school would be out.

"Have you decided yet what you're going to do this summer?" Esther asked, her eyes closed.

174

Rosemary was silent a moment. Then she replied, "No, Esther. This award puts a kind of different light on things."

Esther turned over on her stomach. There was a new facet to her personality since her parents had accepted her marriage—an inner peace which showed in her eyes. She had not had any more sick spells.

"I can hardly wait until exams are over, so Tony and I can move into our apartment. Of course I'm going to miss you, Rosemary."

Rosemary smiled and turned to face her roommate. "You'll be so busy you won't have time to miss me, Esther."

Esther swung her feet over the side of the bed. "Maybe, but I'm sure I'll miss you anyway. Say, we'd better get started if we're going to get any work done tonight."

It was a beautiful night as they hurried across the campus. The full moon hung low over the trees like a huge ripe grapefruit. Rambler roses were in full fragrant bloom on the trellises outside of Howley's. Couples were everywhere, openly ignoring the ban on week-night dating. It was going to be hard concentrating on dry facts, Rosemary thought wistfully. Gray was studying for his first exam the next day. It seemed as though he were always busy, she thought, for he rarely had any leisure time.

Rosemary was still thinking about Gray and was not even aware of someone following them until she heard her name called. It was Lee Ann. She looked as though she had been running.

"Rosemary, could I talk to you a minute?" she asked.

"Why, surely, Lee Ann."

"I'll go on, Rosemary," Esther said with tact. "I'll see you later."

"All right, Esther." Rosemary turned to Lee Ann. "Where did you want to talk?"

"Let's sit down outside, Rosemary. It's such a nice night." They found a bench in front of the Agriculture Building and sat down underneath an elm tree.

"Is something wrong, Lee Ann?" Rosemary asked, studying the other girl's face in the moonlight.

"Not exactly. It's just that my mother called, Rosemary, and she wants me to call her right back. She wants me to fly out to Hollywood as soon as school is out."

"What's wrong with that, Lee Ann?" Rosemary asked, "It sounds scrumptious to me."

Lee Ann's expression was not exactly joyful. "I wanted to go out to Colorado to my Dad's. But Mother says it's her turn since I stayed with Dad last summer." She looked at Rosemary, desperation in her eyes. "Rosemary, I'll be bored to death. Mother's on the set all day. There's not a soul around my own age."

Rosemary said, "Lee Ann, your mother loves you. That's why she wants you to come."

"I suppose so," Lee Ann said. She looked at Rosemary hopefully. "Would you come along? Mother said I could bring a friend for company if I wanted to and she'd pay the fare. I know you don't have any plans made yet, and I'd like to have you anyway. You're the best friend I have at Waverly."

Rosemary stared at Lee Ann. It was an unexpected and an attractive offer. It would be a solution in one way, but it wouldn't provide her with any money for the coming year, and she would have other expenses to meet other than tuition. Besides, if she went to Hollywood, it would disappoint her mother. She would be a whole continent away from Gray, too.

"I'm sorry, Lee Ann," she said, after thinking it over. "I'm truly flattered you would want me, but I simply couldn't go. I'll want to spend time with Mother and I've got to earn some money, too."

Lee Ann looked disappointed, but she said, "I understand, Rosemary. I suppose I'll have to go alone. But maybe it won't be so bad." Her voice quickened. "Do you think we could room together next year, Rosemary?"

"All right, let's," Rosemary said. Lee Ann would be an agreeable roommate.

Lee Ann went back to Lawrence House to return her mother's call and Rosemary went on to the library.

Rosemary had a letter from her mother the next day when she returned from taking her English final exam.

> . . . Jesse wants you to come, too, so please do. Don't feel that you're intruding. Jesse says you can help him out in the school office and earn a little money that way. I really don't think it would be wise for you to say there at Lawrence House alone this summer. You'd be lonely with all of your friends gone. . . .

Rosemary went to the window and stood looking out over the campus. Her mother was right, as usual. It would be lonely, and Gray had already warned her he would have little time to drive over during the summer. Besides, he would have to hoard his money for next year, he had said. Every penny would be important. He wouldn't have much money for dates.

Rosemary reread her mother's letter and was overpowered with a great longing to see her again. Suddenly things fell into place as though Rosemary had found the lost piece of a jigsaw puzzle. She had been uncertain so long, but now she knew what she would do. She was so excited at her decision that she went to Nancy's room to tell her.

Nancy was studying at her worktable. Rosemary told her what she had decided. "I'm glad, Rosemary," she said. "I don't know why you had any qualms, anyway, about spending the summer in Iowa. You said yourself you liked your stepfather and he seemed to like you."

"I know I did, Nancy. I thought I'd be a fifth wheel, something like Cynthia," Rosemary confessed.

Nancy laughed. "Now you sound just like her, and you know how queer she used to be."

Rosemary laughed. Nancy could always jolly her out of everything. "Well, I'm going to Iowa, Nancy. It's final now. I'll tell Mr. Lawrence I won't be wanting my room after all."

She went downstairs to tell him. "You're doing the right thing, Miss Rossiter," he said when she had finished. "Your mother would have been unhappy if you'd stayed here all summer." He reached into his desk and drew out a letter. "Here's something you'll be interested in seeing."

Rosemary noted the expensive stationery and the heading. As her eyes traveled down the typed lines, she knew her face must be registering her astonishment. The letter said:

Dear Mr. Lawrence,

This letter is to thank you for the wonderful visit I had at Lawrence House. I could see that my daughter is in good hands.

I was so impressed with you and your girls and the Waverly campus that I have established (anonymously) a fund for a good citizenship award. I don't want to embarrass my daughter by calling it by my name as long as she is at the college. Daughters can get some odd ideas sometimes, and I know my daughter doesn't always approve of me anyway.

But I hope, after Lee Ann's graduation, it will become known as the Melissa Meadows Award for Good Citizenship. I wanted you, at least, to know what I had done and that it was your house and you who had inspired it.

Rosemary lifted her eyes. "Does Lee Ann know about this, sir?"

He shook his head. "I haven't told anyone else, Miss Rossiter, and don't intend to. But I thought you would like to know the name of your benefactor. I'm afraid Melissa Meadows has been misjudged by a great many people, perhaps most of all by her own daughter."

Rosemary agreed wholeheartedly. "I won't say anything, Mr. Lawrence, and I do appreciate your confidence."

He shook hands with her solemnly, as though he would not see her again at suppertime. "Lawrence House is proud to have you, Rosemary." She realized that he never before had called her by her first name. "We'll be looking forward to your coming back next year."

Rosemary would have liked to kiss him, but you just didn't become that familiar with Irving Lawrence, so she said merely, "I'll be back. Don't worry about that, sir."

Gray took Rosemary to the train. She was wearing a new light-blue suit and the little blue hat she had worn to her mother's wedding. He had brought her a pink rosebud for her lapel. As he carried her bags to the open platform, his brown hair ruffled in the breeze. Rosemary looked up at him, trying to memorize his features. It would be three long months before she saw Gray again. Would he change in that time in his feelings about her? She was sure that she wouldn't change about him no matter what happened.

Gray stood looking down at her rather wistfully. For once his gray eyes weren't twinkling. "I'll be leaving town right away, too, Rosemary," he said. "Dad's coming in an hour to pick me up. Then off to Dr. Fosdick's and to work."

She nodded. "I'll be starting work right away, too, but it's going to make the summer fly by, Gray. It'll be no time at all until fall comes again."

He took her hand and touched each finger gently. "I promise to write every week—to tell you all about the pooches."

"And I'll write all about Iowa, Gray," she said, feeling a lump in her throat.

They heard the train whistling down the track. "Say hello to your mother and Mr. Fisher for me," he said. "I wish I could get out to see you, but it's going to be impossible, Rosemary." He touched her lips gently with his and she felt the tears gathering behind her eyelids, but she made herself smile.

"Good-by, Rosemary," he said.

Gray must remember her smiling, she kept telling herself. Men didn't like women who cried.

"Only till September, Gray," she said gaily. "So it's not really good-by at all." He kissed her once more.

The train ground to a stop beside them. Rosemary stepped on and in a moment it started up again. She waved her handkerchief until Gray was only a tiny dot on the Waverly platform.